卡夫卡
變形記
The Metamorphosis

中英雙語典藏版

法蘭茲‧卡夫卡(Franz Kafka)——著

李毓昭——譯　楊宛靜——繪

—— 收錄 ——

〈變形記〉、〈飢餓藝術家〉

〈二十世紀最偉大的捷克文學家：作家生平解析〉

晨星出版

目錄

CONTENTS

變形記

第 1 章

一天早上，格勒果‧撒摩札從不愉快的夢中醒來，發現自己變成了一隻醜陋的大蟲。他硬如鐵甲的背躺在床上，把頭稍稍抬起來，就看到褐色圓拱的肚皮，分成一節節硬梆梆的弓形肌肉，高突的肚子使蓋在上面的棉被無法固定，感覺就快滑下去了。

與偌大的身軀相比，一對又一對的腳顯得特別細小可憐，在他眼前無力地揮動。

他心想：「我是怎麼了？」這不是夢。

他的房間雖窄小了些，但還是人住的房間，靜置在四面熟悉的牆壁之間。桌上仍擱著尚未收拾好的布料樣品——撒摩札是布料推銷員——桌前的牆上掛著一幅畫，那是他最近從圖畫雜誌上剪下來的，裝在金黃色的相框裡，畫裡是一個婦人，頭戴毛皮帽子，圍著毛皮圍巾，端坐在椅子上，對著看畫的人舉起遮住她整條手臂的暖手筒。

接著，格勒果的眼睛轉向窗口，天空陰沉沉的，傳來雨滴打在窗檯上的聲音，這使他感到憂鬱極了。他心想，乾脆再多睡一會兒，把這件無聊事全部忘掉，可是他睡不著，因為他習慣往右邊側躺，而在目前的情況下，他根本沒有辦法翻身，不論多麼用力向右翻轉，仍舊改變不了仰臥的睡姿。他起碼嘗試了一百次，雙眼緊閉，不想看到自己那些扭動掙扎的腳，但最終還是得斷了翻身的念頭，因為他的腹側開始感到從未有過的隱痛。

他心想：「天啊，我選了一個多麼辛苦的工作啊！每天在路上奔波，成交壓力比在總部辦公要來得大多了，再加上旅途勞頓，不僅要煩惱車班、住宿的問題，而且三餐不定，不時還得與人來往，卻從來無法深交。這些惱人的煩事通通都給我滾開！」他覺得肚皮有些癢，於是躺著把身體慢慢拖向床頭，因為這樣比較容易可以把頭抬起來。他找到發癢的地方，那裡圍繞著許多白色的小斑點，他不知道那些斑點是怎麼回事，雖然試圖用一隻腳去搔抓那裡，但是馬上就縮了回來，因為只要一碰到那地方，身體便不自覺地打起寒顫。

他又挪動身軀，恢復原來的姿勢。他心想，這麼早起床會使人變得愚笨。

人是需要睡眠的。別的推銷員過的生活猶如後宮的女人，比如說，我早上回旅館填寫剛接到的訂單時，那幫人才

剛坐下來吃早餐。如果老闆知道我做了這種事，一定會當場把我開除。不過，那對我未嘗不是件好事，誰知道呢？假如不是顧慮到父母，我早就不幹了。我會到老闆面前，一口氣說出對他的看法，讓他嚇得從桌子上跌下來！他那種作風也真古怪，高坐在桌子上對部屬說話，尤其是老闆有重聽，跟他講話必須靠得很近。但凡事還是有希望的，只要我存夠錢還清父母欠老闆的債——也許再過五、六年——我一定辦得到的。到時候我會把握機會。可是，現在我得起床了，火車五點就要開了。

他看了看五斗櫃上滴答滴答響的鬧鐘。他想，老天爺，已經六點半了。指針持續悄悄地往前走，甚至超過一半，即將指向四十五分了。鬧鐘沒有響嗎？從床上可以看到，鬧鐘確實設定在四點，想必是響過了。可是，他怎麼可能沒有聽到那震耳欲聾的鬧鈴而睡過頭了呢？不，他雖睡得不安穩，但顯然相當熟睡。唉，現在怎麼辦呢？下一班火車是七點。

要搭上那班車，他必須趕緊出發。

可是樣品還沒有收拾好，心情也不怎麼暢快。就算他趕上了那班火車，也無法避免老闆的一頓責罵，因為公司的雜工會去等五點的火車，應該早就去跟老闆報告說他沒有出現。這個雜工是老闆的走狗，既窩囊又愚蠢。那麼，說他生病好了？可是這麼說觸霉頭，而且會令人起疑，畢竟他工作

五年來，從來沒有生過病。老闆一定會親自帶著健保公司的醫生來找他，然後責怪他的父母，說他們的兒子偷懶，而且不管怎麼解釋，老闆也只會採信醫生的說詞。這個醫生認為，所有人都身心健全但怠惰職責，而照目前的情形來看，可以說醫生的這個想法是錯的嗎？除了久睡後遲遲未退去的睡意外，格勒果的身體很健康，他甚至食慾大開。

儘管他非常快速地思考這些，他卻還不能下定決心離開床鋪。鬧鐘走到六點四十五分時，床頭邊的門傳來輕輕的敲門聲。

「格勒果，」有道聲音說，是他的母親。「六點四十五分了，你不是要趕火車嗎？」

好溫柔的聲音！格勒果聽到自己回應的聲音時嚇了一跳，那無疑是他的聲音，的確是，但是夾雜著糾纏不清的唧唧顫聲，好像一股暗流，在話裡面反射縈繞，使得他說的話只在剛開始的瞬間聽得清楚，後面的聲音便被破壞殆盡，所以不能確定對方是否聽得清楚。

格勒果本來想詳細回答，把一切解釋清楚，可是在這樣的情況下，他只能這麼說：「好，好，感謝媽，我現在就起床。」

兩人之間隔著木門，在外面大概聽不出來格勒果的聲音變了，因為母親聽到他的話就放心拖著步伐離開了。然而，這段簡短的談話卻使其他家庭成員注意到格勒果還在家裡，他們覺得很意外。父親此刻正在敲他的側門，很輕，卻是用拳頭敲的。

「格勒果！格勒果！」父親叫道：「你怎麼了？」但過了一會兒後，他再次聲音低沉地催促格勒果起床。「格勒果！格勒果！」

「格勒果，你還好嗎？需不需要什麼東西？」在另一頭，妹妹也輕敲著門問道。

「我很快就好了。」格勒果同時回答他們，費力地留意自己的發音，他在每個字之間停頓，以免聲音聽起來不尋常。父親回去吃早餐了，妹妹卻又低聲說：「格勒果，把門打開，開開門吧。」可是，他根本不想開門，還慶幸自己在旅行中養成了謹慎的習慣，一定會在夜裡鎖上所有的門，就連在家也一樣。

他第一個打算是靜靜起身穿上衣服，不受任何人打擾，先去吃早餐，吃完後再去想要做什麼。他心裡明白，躺在床上胡思亂想也得不到什麼好結果。他記得之前躺在床上常常會感覺到些微的痠痛，可能是睡姿不對的緣故，可是一旦下了床，就會知道那不過是心理作用。所以他迫切地期待這天早上的幻想逐漸消退。

卡夫卡變形記

　　他的聲音改變並不算什麼，那只是重感冒的前兆，跑業務的人常會有這種職業病。他對這一點深信不疑。

　　要甩開棉被很容易，他只需稍稍鼓起身體，棉被就自然掉落了。但下一個動作就難了，尤其是他的軀體寬大得超乎尋常。他需要臂部和手掌來撐起自己，現在身上卻只有細小的腳不斷往四面八方揮動，一點都無法掌控。他想要彎曲其中一隻腳，那隻腳卻第一個伸得直直的，好不容易使那隻腳就範了，其他的腳卻更加瘋狂地揮舞，顯得極為躁動。「躺在床上無所事事也不是辦法。」格勒果自言自語著。

　　他心想，他可以先使下半身離開床鋪，可是他既沒瞥見過自己的下半身，也無從想像它的樣貌，移動起來相當地困難，而移動速度又如此緩慢，最後他憤怒了，不加思索使盡全力甩開身體，卻弄錯了方向，重重地撞到床鋪的下緣，劇痛使他察覺到，下半身目前似乎是他身體最敏感的部位。

　　於是他設法先將自己的上半身搬離床鋪，小心翼翼地把頭移向床邊。

　　這個動作還算簡單，畢竟身軀雖然龐大，至少還能隨著頭部緩慢地移動。然而，好不容易將頭伸到床沿懸空時，他卻害怕得不敢動作，因為按照這姿勢從床上跌下來，除非奇蹟出現，否則他的頭一定會受傷。他現在無論如何都不能昏厥，特別是現在，不然他寧可留在床上。

　　然而，反覆努力了好幾次後，他還是只能躺回原來的位置，嘆了一口氣，轉而看向正互相纏鬥的纖細小腳，戰況猛烈得更勝以往，即便能制止，他也沒有辦法平息這自發性的混亂。他再次告訴自己，留在床上不是辦法，就算離開這裡的希望渺茫，他也要不顧一切地去嘗試，這是最合理的做法。於此同時，他並沒有忘記提醒自己要冷靜，要絕對的冷靜，這比被逼急而草率抉擇要好得多。他盡可能將雙眼聚焦在窗外的風景，但不幸的是，晨霧遮蔽了對面狹窄的街道，這般慘澹的景色沒能帶給他更多的勇氣與慰藉。「七點了，」他聽見鬧鐘再次響起，「都七點了，霧還這麼濃。」他靜靜躺了一會兒，非常輕微地呼吸著，彷彿期望澈底的靜止能使這荒謬的一切恢復原狀。

　　但這時他開始自言自語：「在七點十五分之前，我無論如何都要下床。到時候一定會有人從辦公室過來找我，因為不到七點，那裡就開門了。」他立刻有節奏地搖晃整個身軀，希望把自己搖落至床下。

　　如果他以這個方法下床，只要把頭部抬高，摔下來時就不會受傷。他的背部似乎相當堅硬，掉落在地毯上應該不至於受傷。最讓他擔心的是，此舉必定會產生巨大的聲響，致使房門外的每個人即便沒受到驚嚇，也會相當擔心。不過，他還是得試試。

他已經有一半的身體離開了床鋪。這個新方法與其說是辛苦事，還不如說是個遊戲，因為他只需要前後搖晃自己就可以了。這時他才想到，如果有人可以幫忙，事情就容易多了。兩個強健有力的人——他想到父親和女傭——這兩人就綽綽有餘了。他們只要將手伸進他隆起的背部下方，接著將他搬離床上，屈身放下，然後耐心地留意他是否翻身就大功告成了，但願這些小腳到了地面就能發揮作用。可是，姑且不論所有房門都鎖著，他應該向家人求救嗎？雖然處境悽慘，他想到這一點時，卻不禁莞爾。

他繼續搖晃，搖得越來越猛，快要不能保持平衡了，他得快點做出最後的決定，因為再過五分鐘就是七點十五分——就在這時，大門的門鈴響了。「辦公室派人來了。」他自言自語著，全身近乎僵硬，唯有身上那些細腳們揮舞得愈發快速。一時間，四周悄無聲息。

「他們不會去開門。」格勒果對自己說，內心緊緊抓住這可笑的冀望。

女傭當然一如往常踏著沉重的步伐去開門了。格勒果只聽到訪客道早安的第一個字，就立刻知道來者何人——是經理本人。我究竟造了什麼孽？在這家公司工作，稍微失職就得被這樣懷疑不可？難道所有公司的員工無一不是無賴？難道公司裡面沒有一個忠誠的人？這個人只不過在早上浪費了

公司一個多小時的時間，就得遭受嚴厲的良心譴責，以至他真的神智不清，下不了床？如果有必要了解情況的話，派一個學徒來詢問不就得了。爲何經理必須親自跑這一趟，令他無辜的家人全都知曉，並因此認定此事非比尋常，否則經理爲何非得親自出面才行？

與其說格勒果是下定決心採取行動，不如說是受到這些念頭驅使，他使盡全力從床上甩下來。雖然發出了碰咚響，聲音卻不大。地毯吸收了若干落地聲，他的背也沒有他想像中堅硬，所以那只是一道沉重的聲響，沒有那麼引人注意。不過他不夠小心，沒有將頭抬起，因此撞到了地面；他轉過頭來，在疼痛和惱怒中把頭按在地毯上摩擦。

「有東西掉下來了。」經理在左邊的房間說。

格勒果心裡想著，今天發生在他身上的事或許有一天也會發生在經理身上——沒有人能夠否認這個可能。經理在旁邊的房間以穩重的步伐走了幾步，漆皮靴子吱吱作響，彷彿在草率地回應格勒果的設想。

「格勒果，經理來了。」妹妹在右邊的房間低聲通知他這個情況。

「我知道。」格勒果咕噥著，但不敢將音量提高到足以讓妹妹聽見。

「格勒果，」父親從左邊房間說，「經理先生來了，他想知道為什麼你沒有搭上早班火車。我們不知道該怎麼跟他說。而且經理想要親自當面跟你談。請你把門打開，他不會介意你凌亂的房間。」

「早安，撒摩札先生。」經理這時親切地叫喚他。

當父親還在門邊跟經理說著話，母親對訪客說，「他人不大舒服，經理先生，請相信我。還有什麼原因會使他趕不上火車呢！這孩子滿腦子想的都是工作，晚上都不出門，簡直把我氣壞了。這八天以來他沒有出差，可是每個晚上都待在家裡，只是和我們一起坐在桌邊，不是靜靜地看報紙，就是查對他的出差行程。他唯一的消遣就是做手工藝。譬如，他花了兩、三個晚上做好一個小相框，做得非常精巧，你看到一定會很驚訝，就掛在他的房間裡，等格勒果開門，你就可以看到了。很高興你過來，先生，光靠我們是不能說服他打開門鎖的，他是那麼地頑固。我確定他人不舒服，雖然他早上不是這麼說。」

「我就來了。」格勒果緩慢而謹慎地說著，不過他動也沒有動，因為他怕聽漏了任何一個字。

「我不認為他有別的事由，太太。」經理說，「希望病情不嚴重。但是從另一方面來說，不知道是幸或不幸，為了工作，我們生意人有任何小毛病通常都得忍耐。」

「那麼，經理可以進去了嗎？」父親不耐煩地問道，再次敲打房門。

「不行。」格勒果說。在這聲拒絕後，左邊房間陷入一片尷尬的沉默，而右邊房間裡的妹妹則開始啜泣。

為什麼妹妹不去找其他人？她可能才剛起床，甚至還沒有穿好衣服。那麼，她在哭什麼呢？就因為他不能站起來開門讓經理進去？因為他有可能被炒魷魚？因為老闆會再來向父母索討舊債？但這些可能都不是現在需要操心的。格勒果還在家裡，絲毫沒有棄家不顧的念頭。當然，此刻他躺在地毯上，知道實情的人絕不會真的要他讓經理進來。對於這一點點失禮，以後大可找個藉口搪塞過去，這比被當場解雇要好多。格勒果覺得，目前讓他一個人安靜會比用眼淚、懇求來得聰明。當然，正因為他們什麼都不知道，才會這麼驚慌失措。

「撒摩札，」經理現在大聲叫道，他提高音量，「你是怎麼了？把自己關在房間裡，只用單一個字來答話。你為父母帶來很多不必要的困擾，而且，順帶一提，你還怠惰怠守工作職責，真是不可思議的行為。我要在這裡代表你的父母和老闆，慎重地請你立刻解釋清楚。你令我很驚訝，真的令我相當驚訝，我本以為你是個沉默寡言且深諳事理的人，沒想到會突然做出這般丟臉事。今天早上老闆曾暗示我你曠職的可能原因，是和前陣子託你去收的現金貨款有關，我當時嚴正地跟他發誓那是不可能的。如今，我發現你頑固得令人難以置信，我完全不願再袒護你了，你在公司的職位可不如想像中那般穩當。有些話我本來是想私下告訴你的，可是既然你不必要地浪費我的時間，我想，讓你的父母聽到也無所謂。這陣子你的表現太差了，當然我承認現在是淡季，可是整個年頭沒有一個季節會差到沒業績可做，撒摩札先生，沒有。」

「可是，先生，」格勒果不禁大叫，他激動得忘了一切。「我現在馬上開門。我是因為有一點點不舒服，也覺得頭暈眼花，所以一直起不來。我還躺在床上，可是我覺得好多了。我現在就要下床了，只要再給我一、兩分鐘的時間！我的情況沒有想像中好，但是我沒事，真的。我怎麼會這樣，說病倒就病倒呢？我昨晚還好好的，我父母可以作證，或者說，我那時就有一點預感了，一定有人察覺到我身上出現的徵兆。我應該跟公司報告的！可是我們通常會以為，小毛病用不著請假在家休息。啊，先生，請原諒我的父母！你剛剛責備我的話都是沒有根據的，從沒有人跟我說過那種話。也許你沒有看到我上次交的訂單。不管怎樣，我還是可以搭上八點的火車。多休息了幾個小時，我覺得好多了。先生，別讓我耽誤你的時間，我很快就會去工作，拜託你這麼告訴老闆，替我向他致上歉意。」

　　這番話說得雜亂無章，幾乎聽不出他在說什麼。他不費力地就來到了櫃子旁，也許是多虧了他在床上的練習，現在他試圖靠著櫃子立起身子。他的確想去開門，的確想出去和經理說話。他很想知道，那些堅持要他開門的人，看到他這副模樣時，不知道會說什麼。

　　如果他們很驚駭，那麼他就不用管了，大可以安下心來。但如果他們坦然接受，他也就沒有理由不高興，快點趕去車站，或許還能搭上八點的火車。

　　起初他從磨光的櫃子表面滑下來幾次，最後他用力一蹬，一鼓作氣站了起來。他不再去注意下半身的疼痛，不管那裡痛得多麼厲害。然後他跌在旁邊的椅背後，用細小的腳攀住邊緣。這麼做使他重新控制住自己，保持安靜，因為現在可以聽聽經理說些什麼了。

　　「你聽得懂那些話嗎？」經理問道，「他應該不會想要愚弄我們吧？」

　　「天啊！」母親喊著，流下淚水。「也許他病得很重，我們卻在折磨他。葛蕾特！葛蕾特！」她大叫。

　　「什麼事，媽媽？」妹妹從另一邊叫道。兩人隔著格勒果的房間互相喊話。

　　「妳趕快去請醫生來，格勒果病了。去叫醫生，快點。

妳沒有聽到他怎麼說話嗎？」

「那是動物的聲音。」和母親激動的聲音比起來，經理的聲調平穩許多。

「安娜！安娜！」父親拍著手叫道，聲音穿過玄關傳到廚房。「馬上去找鎖匠來！」

兩個年輕女孩已經跑過玄關，裙子發出了沙沙聲。妹妹怎麼會這麼快就穿好衣服了？然後前門開了。沒有聽到門重新關上的聲音，顯然她們讓門敞開著，就像一般人家發生重大事故時的做法。

不過現在格勒果平靜多了。看來，他說的話再也沒有人聽得懂了，雖然他覺得那些話說得很清楚，甚至比之前還清楚，這可能是因為他的聽覺已經習慣了。無論如何，那些人現在都已相信他不對勁，開始想要幫助他了。他們第一時間積極果斷的安排令他感到欣慰。他覺得自己被拉回到人類的圈子，對醫生和鎖匠寄予厚望，卻沒能明確地辨別兩者的差異竟是這般雲泥之別。為了使聲音盡可能地清晰，也為即將來臨的談話做準備，他咳了一聲，當然是盡可能小聲，因為也許連咳嗽聲都異於人類的聲音了。他再也不相信自己下的決定了。與此同時，隔壁房間仍是一片寂靜。他的父母可能和經理坐在桌邊輕聲討論，也可能全都靠在門邊傾聽。

　　格勒果慢慢把椅子推向門口，然後放開椅子，扶在門邊支撐自己，他細小的腳跟上有點黏。一番努力之後，在那裡喘了一口氣。接著他想要用嘴巴去轉動門鎖的鑰匙，可惜，他嘴裡似乎沒有牙齒——那他要用什麼去抓鑰匙？——欣慰的是，他的下巴十分有力。在下巴的幫助下，他的確轉動了鑰匙，卻沒有注意到他正在傷害自己，因為嘴裡流出褐色的液體，沿著鑰匙滴在地板上。

　　「你們聽，」經理在隔壁說道，「他在轉動鑰匙了。」

　　這對格勒果是一大鼓勵，可是他們應該全部一起為他打氣，包括他的父母。「加油，格勒果！」他們應該大喊，「加油，繼續轉動鑰匙！」想像他們都在注意他的努力，他使盡全力用下巴咬緊鑰匙。隨著鑰匙的旋轉，他也在鎖孔邊旋轉，現在只靠嘴巴支撐全身，他必須用全身的重量去壓鑰匙，或是把它拉下來。最後喀嚓一聲，鎖開了，格勒果精神一振。他吁了一口長氣，自言自語說：「用不著鎖匠了。」然後把頭放在門把上，把整道門打開。

　　他必須把房門拉向自己，因為即便門已然敞開，卻還看不見他的身體。他得慢慢繞過門緣，而且要非常小心，以免猛然把背摔在門檻上。他繼續進行這項艱鉅的任務，沒有時間去注意別的事情。但在這時，他突然聽見經理大叫一聲——聽起來好像一陣大風。現在他看到經理了，經理站在離門邊最近的地方，用手掩住合不攏的嘴，慢慢往後退，宛如被某種無形的力量持續驅迫。雖然經理在這裡，他母親的頭髮卻沒有梳理，鬆散雜亂。她起初雙手合十，看著他父親，然後朝格勒果前進兩步，隨即倒在她攤開的裙子上，臉垂在胸前，完全看不見了。父親緊握著拳頭，臉上帶著兇猛的表情，好像要把格勒果打回房間，然後不安地張望客廳，用雙手矇住眼睛，隨即哭了出來，寬闊的胸膛上下起伏著。

格勒果沒有進到客廳，而是倚在另一片緊閉的門上，所以他只露出一半的身體，偏著頭看著大家。太陽光越來越強了，對街是一排排無止境的灰黑色房子，那是醫院，從這裡可以清楚看到其中一部分，有一排莊嚴整齊的窗戶點綴著。雨還在下，但只看得見大雨粒一滴滴地往下掉。早餐的碗盤擺滿了桌子，因為格勒果的父親認為，早餐是一天之中最重要的，他會在那裡耗上幾個小時，看各種各樣的報紙。正對著格勒果的牆壁上掛著他當兵時的照片，他是個中尉，手擱在佩劍上，臉上帶著愉快無憂的笑容，令人對他的制服和軍人儀態產生敬意。通往玄關的門半開著，大門也敞開著，可以一直看到前廊和往下走的臺階。

「那麼，」格勒果清楚意識到自己是唯一保持鎮定的人，「我會立刻穿上衣服，整理好樣品出門。你們要讓我去嗎？你看到了，先生，我並不頑固，我很願意工作；出差旅行很辛苦，但是不這麼做我就活不下去。先生，你要去哪

裡？回辦公室嗎？你能不能如實替我解釋這一切？誰都會偶
爾不能工作，但是這個時候會讓人回憶之前的成績，並在日
後牢記在心，等到無法工作的時期結束，他就會以更大的熱
誠和專注力去工作。我願意忠心地服侍老闆，你向來很明瞭
這點，何況我必須扶養父母和妹妹。我的處境很艱難，但是
我會克服的。請你不要讓我的處境變得更糟糕，在公司為我
說說好話吧。業務員在那裡不受歡迎，我知道。別人以為業
務員收入豐厚，而且生活安逸。沒有特別的因素可以改變這
樣的偏見，可是先生，你比其他職員看得更清楚，是的，我
可以肯定地說，你看得比老闆還清楚，老闆很容易對某個員
工做出不正確的判斷。而你是知道的，業務員幾乎一整年都
不會在辦公室出現，很容易成為流言、噩運或顧客無故抱怨
的犧牲者，而他卻完全無法為自己辯解，因為他全都被矇在
鼓裡，等到他精疲力盡，結束旅程回來，才會親身經歷到那
些事情的苦果，卻已經無法去追究緣由了。先生，先生，別
一聲不響地離開啊，至少請你表示，你相信我說的話有一部
分是事實！」

　　可是格勒果才剛開口說話，經理就轉身了，現在他張嘴
回頭瞪著格勒果，肩膀顫抖著。而且在格勒果說話時，他沒
有一刻是停止不動的，他一邊盯著格勒果一邊走向門口，但
非常緩慢，好像在遵從某道要他離開的祕令。他已經走到玄
關了，只差一步就要離開客廳時，動作突兀得令人以為他的

腳跟燒了火。他一進入玄關，右手臂就伸向前方的臺階，好像有一股超能力在那裡解救了他。

格勒果知道，絕不能讓經理在這種心態下離開，特別是現在自己在公司的職位岌岌可危。父母並不太了解這一點，他們多年來早已相當篤定格勒果會在這公司待一輩子，何況他們所有的心思都放在眼前的問題上，沒有任何遠見。不過，格勒果有，所以無論如何都得挽留經理，安慰、說服他，使他肯為自己說話。格勒果和全家的未來就看這一時了！真希望妹妹在這裡！她很聰明，格勒果還靜靜躺在床上時，她就開始哭了，而經理向來對女人都很心軟，一定會被妹妹給說服。她會關上公寓的大門，在玄關化解經理的驚恐。可是她不在這裡，格勒果必須自行處理這個情況。

他沒想到自己都還不知道擁有什麼樣的行動能力，也忘記他的話有可能，不！十之八九都沒辦法讓人聽懂，居然就離開了門邊，奮力經過通道，往經理那裡走去，而經理已經用雙手攀住平臺上的欄杆，顯得很滑稽。格勒果馬上想要找地方支撐，卻發出微弱的叫聲，跌在眾多細小的腳上面，直到這一瞬間，他才覺得今天早上第一次有了舒適感。他的腳有穩固的底部，而且百依百順，他欣喜地發現這個事實。那些腳甚至努力依他意思前進，他不禁覺得，所有折磨都快要結束了。可是當他在地板上平心靜氣地移動著，晃過接近他母親身邊時，原本陷在衣裙裡的她，忽然一躍而起，退得遠遠地並伸出手指大叫：「救命，老天啊，救命！」她一度低下頭，好像要把格勒果看個仔細，於此同時又無意識地往後退，全忘了擺滿早餐的桌子就在後面，倉促地一屁股坐下去，一副茫然的模樣，似乎也沒有留意到一旁的大咖啡壺傾倒了，壺裡的咖啡潑灑至地毯上。

「媽，媽！」格勒果低聲說著，抬頭看著她。他這時已經把經理忘在一邊，看著流淌下的咖啡，嘴巴不禁啪啪地開闔了起來。如此又讓他的母親出聲大叫，跳開那張桌子，撲進聞聲趕來的丈夫懷裡。可是格勒果現在沒有時間去顧慮父母親了，經理已經走下臺階，踉蹌地趴在欄杆上移動著，轉過頭瞥了最後一眼。格勒果情急地縱身一跳，竭盡全力想要攔住他，經理似乎有所警覺，跳下好幾級臺階，不見了蹤影，嘴裡還直嚷著「啊」，迴聲響徹整個樓梯間。

不幸的是，經理的逃跑似乎觸發了格勒果父親的怒火，他之前都還很鎮定，這時不僅沒有去追趕經理，也沒有阻止格勒果走出來，反而用右手一把抓起經理遺忘在桌上的帽子、外套和手杖，左手則拾起桌子上的一大張報紙，開始踏步跺腳、揮動手杖和報紙，想把格勒果趕回他的房間。格勒果怎麼哀求都沒用，事實上他的哀求也沒有人聽得懂，不論他怎麼卑屈地低頭，都只讓父親更用力地在地板上跺足。

母親則打開父親後方的那一扇窗，雖然天氣寒冷，她卻

雙手掩面探出窗外。街上颳來一陣強風，湧進樓梯間，窗簾漲滿空氣飛舞著，桌上的報紙啪啪地翻飄著，有幾張飄落到了地板上。格勒果的父親無情地驅趕他，嘴裡還像野蠻人一般嘶嘶叫著。可是格勒果並沒有練習過倒退走，所以他的動作非常緩慢。如果他有機會轉過身，就可以立刻回房，可是他擔心自己慢慢轉身的動作會激怒父親，父親手上的手杖隨時都可能在他的背上或頭部敲下致命的一擊。最後，他別無選擇，因為他驚恐地發現，後退時他連方向都控制不了。只好一邊不安地越過肩膀看向父親，一邊盡可能快速轉身，事實上仍舊相當緩慢。也許父親察覺到他的善意了，並沒有阻撓他轉身，而且彼此即便相隔好一段距離，父親仍好心地用手杖的一端指揮格勒果，幫助他轉身。

如果父親可以停止那種令人難以忍受的嘶嘶聲就好了！

那種聲音使格勒果昏了頭。他已經完全轉過身來了，但嘶嘶不絕於耳，以致搞錯方向，又稍微轉了回來。等到他的頭成功對準敞開的房門，他的身體卻又寬闊得無法通過。父親在目前的情緒下，當然不可能想到可以打開另一扇門，給格勒果足夠的空間通過；他滿心只想著該如何盡快把格勒果趕回房間，絕不可能忍受格勒果慢條斯理地做好準備，他需要先適應自己的體態，然後再穿進門；相反地，父親發出了更古怪的聲音，將格勒果往前推，彷彿前方沒有任何障礙

般。在格勒果身後的噪音，這時聽起來彷彿已不再像是個父
親了，這可不是鬧著玩的，格勒果什麼都顧不得了，死命把
自己擠進門。他抬高一邊身體，隨著門邊傾斜，肚皮都磨疼
了，還在白色的門上留下醜陋的汙漬。他很快就被卡在門
上，無法再靠自己前進，一邊的腳在半空中顫抖，另一邊的
腳則痛苦地壓在地上，直到父親在後面用力一推，他才咻的
直衝進房內，身上淌出大量的血。他後方的門被手杖一抵，
砰然關上，終於恢復了寧靜。

第 2 章

　　到了黃昏，格勒果才從沉睡中醒來。與其說是睡眠，不如說是昏迷。原本他可以再睡久一會兒才自然醒來，不過他休息夠了，也睡得很充足，但是他似乎是被走廊上匆忙的腳步聲，和輕輕關上門的聲響所吵醒的。街燈拋入房的光線，在天花板和家具上方映出慘白的顏色，可是在他躺臥的地方周圍卻是黑暗的。慢慢地，他移動到門邊，初次用觸角笨拙地摸索，看看那裡發生了什麼事。他覺得左側腹好像有一條很不舒服的長條硬痂，而他身上的兩排腳目前只能跛行，其中一隻細腳在早上的事件中遭受重傷，只能無力地在後方拖著，然而只有一隻腳受傷簡直是奇蹟。

　　走到房門邊他才知道是什麼吸引他靠近：食物的香味。那裡擺著一碗滿滿的鮮牛奶，上面漂著切碎的白麵包。他高興得幾乎要笑出聲來，由於肚子比早上更餓，他馬上一頭栽進牛奶裡面，幾乎淹到了眼睛，可是他馬上就失望地抬起頭來。不僅是因為身體左側受傷使他不易進食，一動就痛；加上喘著大氣，身體上下抖動的格勒果，只能找到一個合適的

卡夫卡變形記

角度才能吃上東西。他也不喜歡牛奶的味道，雖然他以前最愛喝牛奶，這也是爲什麼妹妹要給他送來牛奶；事實上，他幾乎是感到厭惡地遠離那只碗，爬回房間中央。

從門縫可以看到，客廳已經亮起煤氣燈，平常在這個時候，父親都習慣用宏亮的聲音唸晚報給母親聽，有時候也唸給妹妹聽，此時卻一點聲音都沒有。妹妹曾在交談時和來信上多次向他提到父親這種大聲唸報紙的習慣，或許父親最近不再這麼做了。可是，四周依舊悄然無聲，儘管這屋裡不可能沒有人。「我們家的生活多麼安靜啊！」格勒果自言自語著。他凝視著眼前的黑暗，他覺得很驕傲，自己供得起父母和妹妹住在這麼美麗的公寓，過這麼好的生活。但是，如果這一切祥和、富裕和幸福的生活，將在此時打上可怕的句點呢？爲了避免在這種思緒中茫然失措，格勒果決定開始移動，在房間裡爬來爬去。

在漫長的傍晚時分，有道側門一度打開了一條縫，但是很快就關上了。不久，另一道側門也是一樣；顯然有人想要進來，卻又改變了主意。格勒果很快地移動到客廳旁的那扇門邊，決心請那猶豫的訪客進來，至少要弄清楚這個人是誰。可是那道門並沒有再度開啟，他白等了。早上門都上鎖時，他們都想要進來，現在他已經開了一扇門，其他的門在白天顯然也都被打開過，卻沒有人進來，連鑰匙都還插在外頭的鑰匙孔上。

　　直到夜深了，客廳的煤氣燈才熄滅，格勒果可以輕易地確認父母和妹妹都還沒睡，因為他清楚聽見他們三個人踮著腳尖離開的聲音。看來在明天早上以前，都不會有人進來找他了，絕對是這樣的，所以將有很長一段時間不會受到干擾，他可以好好重新考慮如何安排往後的生活。可是在這個天花板高懸、空蕩蕩的房間裡，他只能平躺在地板上，心中充滿著無法言說的憂慮，雖然這裡是他五年來住慣的房間。他有意無意地、有些羞愧地鑽進沙發底下，儘管背部稍微卡住，而且沒有辦法抬起頭，他仍就此感到無比舒適。唯一的遺憾是，身體太過於寬大，不能全部塞進沙發下面。

　　他整晚都待在那裡，有些時候是在打盹，但飢餓感不時使他驚醒；有些時候不是滿懷憂慮就是在勾勒模糊的希望，但都得出同樣的結論，那就是他得暫時保持冷靜，對家人展現無比的耐心和寬容的諒解，因為他們得容忍如此樣貌下的他所造成的種種不便。

　　一大清早，天都還沒有亮，格勒果就有機會測試他剛下的決心，因為穿戴整齊的妹妹從玄關開門，焦急地窺探房內。她沒有馬上看到他，但當瞥見他在沙發底下時，她無法遮掩住驚恐，嚇得啪的一聲把門關上。天啊！他總會在某處啊，難道他溜得掉？但妹妹好像對自己的行徑感到後悔，她馬上又打開門，踮著腳尖進來，彷彿在探訪重病患者或陌生人。格勒果把頭伸到沙發邊緣，注視著她。她會不會發現牛奶原封不動並不是因爲他肚子不餓，而改帶其他較合他口味的食物來？除非她自己察覺到，否則他寧可餓死，也不會爲了讓她察覺眞相而引起她注意，儘管他此時有股很強烈的衝動，想要從沙發下跳出來，伏在她的腳下，求她拿好吃的東西來。可是妹妹一下子就明白了，她很驚訝那碗牛奶還是滿滿的，只有一點點濺在旁邊。她立刻把碗拿起來，但不是直接用手，而是隔著一塊布，然後就離開了。格勒果迫切想要知道她會改帶來什麼食物，他幻想著不同食物的畫面。她果眞給他帶來食物了，出自她的一片好心，卻是格勒果絕對猜不到的東西。爲了試探他的喜好，她帶來許多種食物，全擺在一張舊報紙上，上面有半爛的蔬菜，有昨天晚餐吃剩的骨頭，上面還裹著幾乎凝固的白色醬汁；幾顆葡萄乾和杏仁；一片格勒果兩天前說很難吃的乳酪；還有一塊乾麵包、一塊塗了奶油的麵包捲，以及一塊塗了奶油的鹹麵包。不僅如此，她還擺上了一個碗，裡面有一些水，顯然那個碗是要給他專用的。善解人意的她也知道格勒果不會在她面前吃東西，放下食物後就迅速離開，還用鑰匙上了鎖，這等於是在告訴他，他大可以隨心所欲地吃。格勒果的小腳們一齊窸窸窣窣地跑向食物，而且他的傷口一定已經癒合了，因爲他沒有再感覺到任何不方便，這讓他很訝異，想到一個月前他只是用刀子稍微割傷了手指，卻直到前天還會痛。

我是不是會越來越不敏感？他想。接著便貪婪地吸吮乳酪,那是所有食物中最吸引他的。一樣接著一樣,他快速地吞食乳酪、蔬菜和醬汁,滿足得流下淚來。至於新鮮的食物,他倒是沒什麼興趣,他甚至不能忍受它們的氣味,還得把他想吃的東西銜到遠一點的地方吃。當妹妹慢慢轉動鑰匙,暗示他退開時,他早已滿足地、懶懶地躺在原處。雖然都快睡著了,他還是被聲響嚇得立刻跳起來,趕緊躲回到沙發底下。可是要待在那下面需要相當的自制力,雖然妹妹在房間裡逗留的時間很短,但他的身體因為飽餐一頓而變得比較臃腫,侷促的空間使他幾乎不能呼吸,好幾次喘不過氣來,盯視妹妹的眼睛開始有點暴突,妹妹卻毫不知情地用掃帚把他吃過的菜,甚至連同他根本沒碰過的東西也掃在一起,好像那些東西都沒有用了,然後快速鏟起來倒進桶子裡,蓋上木頭蓋子後就拎出房間了。妹妹一轉過身,格勒果就從沙發下鑽出,伸伸懶腰,讓身體鼓脹起來。

格勒果就這樣每天都有食物吃,一大早就可以先吃一餐,在父母和女傭都還在睡覺的時候;另一餐是在家人用過午飯以後,父母如以往都會睡個午覺,而女傭會被妹妹派出去跑腿辦事。當然父母並不希望他餓死,但也許除了從妹妹那裡打聽之外,他們並不想親眼看見他吃些什麼,而妹妹也希望盡可能減少他們的哀傷,畢竟他們已經承受夠多了。

那天早上他們是如何把醫生和鎖匠打發走的,格勒果無從知道,因為自從他的話無法讓家人聽懂以後,包括妹妹在內，沒人預料得到他還聽得懂他們說的話，所以當妹妹回到自己的房間，只要能偶爾聽到她發出歎息聲，或是向聖者祈禱的話語，他就該感到滿足了。後來，在她越來越習慣這一切後——當然她永遠無法完全習慣——她有時候會講出帶有善意或相似意圖的話來。

「嗯，他喜歡今天的晚餐。」她會在格勒果把食物吃光的時候這麼說，而在他沒有吃時——這種情況越來越多——她就會幾近悲傷地說：「又全部剩下來了。」

但儘管格勒果無法直接聽到消息，他還是可以從隔壁房間聽到很多話聲，一聽見有人說話，他就會跑到相鄰的那扇門邊，全身貼在上面。尤其是頭幾天，沒有一次談話與他無關，縱使是私下的對話。整整兩天，家人用餐時都會商量該怎麼辦，而就算不是吃飯時間，他們也會討論同樣的話題，因為家裡至少都會有兩個成員在，沒有人願意單獨留在家裡，卻又不能讓屋裡空無一人。在事情發生的第一天，廚娘都還不清楚發生了什麼事，或怎麼發生的，就跪地懇求母親准許她離開，而過了十五分鐘，她就流著眼淚道謝辭別，好像這家人解僱她是莫大的恩惠，還在沒有人要求的情況下發重誓說，她絕不會把這件事洩露出去，隻字不提。

現在格勒果的妹妹也得幫母親下廚了，不過，做飯並不費事，因為他們都沒有胃口。格勒果經常聽到某個家人勸另一個人多吃，但都沒用，得到的回覆總是「謝謝，我吃飽了」之類的話。他們可能也不喝酒了。妹妹經常會問父親要不要喝點啤酒，並且開心地柔聲說她要去買，然後當父親不答腔時，改口說可以請門房的太太幫忙買，以免父親不放心，但這時父親就會大聲說「不要」，接著喝酒的事就沒有人再提起了。

　　事情發生的那天，父親就對母親和妹妹說明家裡的經濟狀況和管理。他不時從桌邊起身，從五年前事業失敗時留下來的小金庫中取出一些憑單或帳簿。這時可以聽到他打開複雜的鎖，窸窸窣窣地取出他要找的文件，再把金庫關上。父親當時的說明是格勒果失去自由以來，頭一次聽到的好消息。他原以為父親的事業什麼都沒有留下，至少父親也從沒有提過看似不相符的事情，當然格勒果也不曾直接去問他。當時格勒果唯一的心願，就是盡全力幫助家人早日度過那次的不幸，那不僅毀了父親的事業，也使他們走向絕望的深淵。於是他熱心投入於工作，幾乎是一夕之間，很快就從小助理變成了推銷員，當然這是因為當推銷員的賺錢機會多了許多，他的成功也能立刻看到現金收入，讓他得以擺在桌上，使家人驚喜不已。

　　那是段輝煌的時期，雖然後來格勒果賺了很多錢，足夠維持家計，也確實供給了全家所需，但家人又驚又喜的表情已不復見，至少那時的榮耀已不再有了。他們都習慣了，包括家人和格勒果在內，家人感激地收下錢，格勒果也樂於沉浸其中，但是不再感到特別溫暖。只有妹妹還和他保持親密，她和格勒果不一樣，很喜歡音樂，能拉出動人的小提琴樂曲。格勒果的心中有個計畫，就是讓妹妹明年去上音樂學校，雖然那是一筆偌大的開銷，但必定可以用其他方式來湊足學費。他在家裡短暫停留時，經常與妹妹在談話中提到音樂學校，但只把這件事當成不切實際的美麗夢想，他的父母光是聽到這吃人般的夢話就會垂頭喪氣。然而，格勒果已經謹慎思考過並打定主意，準備在今年耶誕夜正式宣布這件事的。

在他貼著門立起身軀聆聽時，這些思緒在他的腦海中掠過，但是依他目前的情況，一切都變得毫無意義了。有時出於純粹的疲累，他得停止聆聽，把頭砰的隨便靠在門上，但是他通常會立刻振起精神，因為即使只發出一點點聲響，都會讓門外的人聽到，因而中斷談話。

「不曉得他又在做什麼？」過一陣子父親會這麼說，顯然轉身面對著那道門，也唯有這個時候，中斷的談話才會再繼續。

因為父親很久沒有在意過那筆錢了，而母親也經常無法一次就聽懂，所以父親會一遍又一遍地反覆解釋，使格勒果知道他有一筆錢，金額雖不多，卻是他們從過往財務危機中保留下來的，由於一直沒有動用，利息逐年增加。除此之外，格勒果只留幾塊錢給自己花用，其餘的每個月都交給家人，那些錢也一直都沒有全部用完，現在也已累積了一小筆錢。格勒果在門後面激動地不停地點頭，為這種出乎意料的節約和遠見感到欣喜。沒錯，他其實可以用多餘的錢來償還欠老闆的債務，那樣的話格勒果或許可以更快擺脫現狀，但是父親的安排無疑是比較有利的。

然而，這一筆錢絕不足以讓家人靠利息過活，也許夠維持一年，頂多兩年，不能再久了。為了因應不時之需，那筆錢不應該動用才是，生活費必須另外張羅。父親現在雖還很健壯，但年紀大了，而且五年來都沒有工作，能夠做的事也不多。在他辛苦勞累卻失敗的人生中，這五年是他初嘗休息的滋味，因而增肥了許多，行動也很遲緩。至於格勒果的母親，她有氣喘病，現在連在家裡走動都感到吃力，使她每隔一天就要躺在沙發上，在敞開的窗邊喘氣，這樣的她要如何去賺錢呢？難道要叫妹妹去賺錢嗎？她只是個十七歲的女孩，到目前為止都過得很快樂，穿得漂漂亮亮的，睡得晚，偶爾幫忙做家務，除了出門參加幾次不起眼的活動外，都只在家拉小提琴。每次談到需要有人去賺錢，格勒果就會離開門邊，倒在旁邊冷冰冰的皮沙發上，因為羞愧和悲哀而感到全身燥熱。

他經常躺在那裡度過漫漫長夜，徹夜未眠，只是連續幾個小時抓搔著沙發皮。他也會使出全力把扶手椅推到窗邊，爬上窗沿，抵著椅子靠在窗框上向外看，他懷想起以前滿足地望著窗外時的回憶。因為在現實中，即使是近在眼前的景物，也變得一天比一天模糊了。以前覺得對街的醫院太常映入眼簾，令他感到厭惡，現在他的視線裡再也看不到了。而要不是他知道自己住在市內很寧靜的樹羅登街，他可能會以為窗外是塊荒地，灰濛的天空和灰暗的土地融成一片，無法分辨。他聰慧的妹妹一定注意到幾次扶手椅擺在窗邊，所以每次打掃完房間，都會再把椅子推回到窗邊，也不再關上裡窗。

如果能夠跟她說話，謝謝她所做的一切，他會比較能接受她的照顧，畢竟那些照顧令他感到痛苦。妹妹在做這些事情時當然會盡量掩飾她的彆扭，但時間久了就越來越自然，而時間越久也讓格勒果更加感慨。光是她進來的方式就令他難過，她一進來，就要衝到窗邊，連先關上房門都不願意。儘管除此之外她其實都很小心，避免他人窺視格勒果的房間。現在進房後彷彿快要窒息似，匆忙地拉開窗戶，明明外頭寒風刺骨，仍會在窗邊深呼吸一會兒。她的倉皇舉動每天都會讓格勒果驚嚇兩次，令他蜷縮在沙發下發抖。他心裡明白，如果妹妹能夠毫不畏懼地在窗戶緊閉的房間裡與他共處，她當然不願讓他遭受這樣的折磨。

格勒果變形後過了約一個月，妹妹看到他的樣子應該沒有理由再感到害怕。有一次她比平常早了一點打開門，撞見格勒果動也不動地盯著窗外，看來像個就定位嚇人的怪物。如果妹妹沒有進來，格勒果並不會感到意外，畢竟他杵在那裡，妹妹就不能立刻去開窗戶，可是妹妹不僅愣住了，還驚嚇得往後跳砰的甩上門。不認識的人看到，可能會以爲他是故意躺在那裡，等她過來就要去咬她。當然他馬上就跑去躲在沙發底下，但是一直等到中午她才再度前來，而且比平常更加忐忑不安。他終於明白，妹妹仍舊排斥他的模樣，也將會永遠排斥。她即使看到他的一小部分身體在沙發底下露出來，她都要有相當的自制力才不會拔腿就跑。爲了妹妹好，有一天格勒果把一塊布放在背上，帶到沙發上──這花了他四個小時的工夫──使布塊能完全遮住身體，如此一來，就算她蹲下來也看不見他。如果她覺得那塊布並不需要，她當然可以把布塊從沙發上扯下來，因爲很明顯的，把自己完全隔絕並不會讓格勒果感到舒服，可是她並沒有去動布塊，甚至在格勒果用頭小心地掀開布塊，好看看她對這個新布置有什麼反應時，還從她的眼中瞥見了一絲謝意。

在前兩個星期，格勒果的父母無論如何都不敢進入他的房間，他經常聽見他們對妹妹的幫助表示感激，明明在此前他們還不時責備她，認爲女兒一無是處。可是現在，妹妹在打掃他的房間時，父親和母親常常會等在門外，妹妹一出來就要詳實地告訴他們房裡的情形，例如格勒果吃了什麼、這

次他有什麼舉止、他的情況是否有點改善等等。母親很快就
會想要進去看他，可是父親和妹妹用了一些理由來阻止她，
起初格勒果聽得很仔細，也全然同意那些話。但是不久之
後，他們就得用力攔阻母親才行，母親這時會大叫：「讓我
進去看格勒果，他是我可憐的兒子啊！你們不明白我一定得
進去看看他嗎？」格勒果心想，讓她進來也好，當然不必每
天，或許一個星期一次，畢竟她比妹妹還能理解這一切，儘
管妹妹再勇敢，都還只是個孩子，她純粹因為年輕氣盛，才
會魯莽地決定花費心力，承擔如此艱鉅的工作。

　　格勒果想和母親見面的心願很快就實現了。他為了父母
著想，白天不會出現在窗邊，可是在只有幾平方公尺的地板
上，他也爬不了多久；到了晚上，他也無法忍受整晚都靜靜
地躺著不動，加上食物再也無法讓他感到興奮。為了解悶，
他養成了在牆壁和天花板上爬行的習慣。他甚至喜歡懸吊在
天花板上，這比躺在地板上好多了。他可以舒服地呼吸，並
開心地輕晃著身體。令他吃驚的是可能發生這樣的事，當他
幾近興奮地懸在上頭時，他突然把腳放開，掉落到地上。

　　不過現在他可以自然地掌控身體，從空中摔下來也不會
受傷。妹妹立刻就發現了格勒果找到的新消遣，因為他爬過
的地方都會留下腳跟的黏液。她有個念頭，想盡量給他寬敞
的空間爬行，所以必須移開擋路的家具，尤其是櫥櫃和桌
子。

可是她一個人搬不動，又不敢請父親幫忙，至於那個女傭，她僅是個十六歲的女孩子，雖然敢在廚娘離開後留下來，但是要找她幫忙是不可能的，因為她懇求讓她整日待在廚房活動，只有特殊命令時才會打開門回應。唯一的辦法就是趁父親出門時，請母親過來幫忙。

走向格勒果的房門時，母親還興奮地叫喊著，但是一到門邊她就沉默了。格勒果的妹妹當然先進去，確定裡面的一切都沒問題，才讓母親進去。格勒果慌忙把布塊拉低，布塊在地面擠出皺褶，看起來就像是隨便丟在沙發上的床罩。格勒果選擇後退，不從布的下面窺看，他忍住看媽媽一眼的渴望，只要母親肯來，他就很高興了。

「進來，他躲起來了。」妹妹說道，顯然是牽著母親進來的。格勒果聽見兩個孱弱的女人在努力搬開沉重的舊櫃子，妹妹總是擔負較費力的工作，不顧母親的勸告，母親擔心她會拉傷。

過了好久，至少有十五分鐘，母親就說最好讓櫃子留在原地，第一個原因是它太重，她們絕不可能在父親回來前搬好，而如果把櫃子留在房間中央，只會阻礙格勒果的活動路徑；第二個原因是，她們並不知道移動家具是否會讓格勒果開心。她的想法與妹妹相反，空蕩蕩的牆壁像把利刃刺穿她的心，也許格勒果的感覺也是一樣，畢竟這麼久以來他對這些家具已經相當習慣，沒有了家具，他也許會感到被遺棄。

　　她的話聲很輕，事實上她一直在悄聲說話，好像連聲音都不想讓格勒果聽見，因為她相信兒子已經聽不懂她說的話，儘管她並不知道兒子身在哪裡。她平靜地下了結論：「我們如果把他的家具搬走，看起來不就像是我們對他的復元不再抱持希望，打算冷酷地把他留在這嗎？我想最好讓他的房間保持原狀，這麼一來，等他回到我們身邊時，他會發現一切都沒有改變，就會比較容易忘掉這之間發生的不愉快。」

　　聽到母親這番話，格勒果了解到，過去兩個月以來，完全沒有與人直接對話，加上單調乏味的家庭生活，一定使他腦子不正常了，否則他不會這麼希望房間沒有家具，變得空蕩蕩的。這個房間很溫暖，用祖傳的家具布置得很舒適，他真的希望這個房間變成空無一物的巢穴，讓他可以不受阻礙地四處爬行，卻同時在一瞬間遺忘所有身為人類的記憶嗎？他是否就快要拋棄這一切了？唯有久未聞見的母親聲音讓他重拾回憶。房間的每一樣東西都不應該搬走，每樣東西都要維持原位，少了家具帶來的良好益處他可無法生活，就算家具會妨礙他愚蠢地四處爬行，那不僅無害，反而有絕大的優點。

　　可惜妹妹的想法全然不同，她在和父母說起格勒果的事時，已經習慣以專家自居，雖然那不是沒有原因的，但母親的忠告反而令她擁有充足的理由下定決心，不僅要搬走原本想到的櫃子和書桌，除了不可缺少的沙發之外，所有家具都必須搬走。當然她會如此堅決，不純粹是出於孩子氣的反抗心理，也不是因為辛苦照顧遭遇變故的哥哥而獲得的自信：她實際上察覺到，格勒果需要許多爬行的空間，而且就目前的情況看來，他根本用不著家具。還有一個影響她，並促使她這麼做的重大因素，即是少女對事物的熱忱。如今的葛蕾特試圖將哥哥的情況變得更嚴峻，這樣她就能為他做更多事。在格勒果單獨占據的空房間裡，除了她自己，將不會再有任何人敢進去了。

所以，母親沒辦法勸退她，使她改變心意。現在母親在格勒果的房間裡似乎更為焦躁不安了，她不知如何是好，也就不再開口，只是盡力幫女兒把櫃子推出房外。格勒果可以接受房裡沒有櫃子，但是書桌一定要留住。兩個女人把櫃子推出門外，邊推邊呻吟時，格勒果從沙發底下伸出頭來，想著如何盡可能和善而慎重地阻止她們。可是運氣不好，他的母親先走了回來，葛蕾特在隔壁房間雙手環繞著櫃子，打算自己努力晃動它，當然櫃子不動如山。母親還不習慣看見格勒果的模樣，他可能會把她嚇壞了，格勒果猛然縮回沙發的另一頭，布塊前端因而滑動了一點。這就足以引起母親的注意了，她頓時停下腳步，靜止不動一會兒，隨即走回葛蕾特那裡。

　　雖然格勒果一直在安慰自己，沒什麼大不了的，只是移動了幾件家具，但是不久便發現，這兩個女人進進出出的腳步聲，輕聲細語的交談聲，和家具磨著地板發出的嘎嘎擦聲，他彷彿被四面八方而來的噪音給吞噬。無論他怎麼把頭和腳緊縮在地板上，他還是得承認，再這樣下去他會受不了。她們想要搬空他的房間，拿走所有他珍惜的東西。裝著鋼絲鋸和其他工具的櫃子已經搬走了，她們正在鬆脫鎖匙，因為書桌被牢牢固定在地板上。他的所有作業都是在那張桌子上完成的，在他唸商專、唸中學，甚至還在上小學時都是。他沒有時間去揣測那兩個女人的善意，他現在甚至忘了她們的存在。因為搬得非常疲倦，她們已不發一語，除了啪嗒啪嗒的沉重腳步聲之外，什麼都聽不到。

　　於是當她們將書桌搬到了隔壁房間，靠在書桌上喘著氣休息時，他快步衝了出來，一下轉向東，一下轉向西，再轉向南與北，實在不知道要先救哪樣物品。這時，他在已無家具擺放的牆壁上，看到那幅穿戴許多毛皮的婦人照片，他快速爬到那裡，身體貼在鑲嵌著照片的玻璃上，正好可以冷卻他發燙的肚皮。照片完全被他遮住了，至少這樣東西不會被拿走。他把頭轉向客廳的門，看看她們是不是回來了。

　　她們沒有休息多久就進來了，葛蕾特的手臂圍在母親身上，緊緊摟著她走。「我們現在要搬哪一樣？」葛蕾特張望四周說著，接著她與牆上的格勒果四目交視。或許是因為母親在場，她還能泰然自若，她看向母親的臉龐，即時阻止母親發現，然後以顫抖的聲音脫口說道：「這樣吧，我們先回客廳再休息一會兒，好嗎？」格勒果很清楚妹妹想怎麼做，她想先把母親帶到安全的地方，再過來把他從牆上趕走。好，她儘管試試看！他會緊緊抓住照片，絕不放手。他寧可飛到葛蕾特的臉上，也不要失去照片。

可是葛蕾特的話反而令母親心神不安，母親往旁邊走了一步，瞥見花紋壁紙上有個偌大的褐色塊狀物，還沒有意識到她看到的就是格勒果，便用嘶啞的聲音大叫：「天啊，天啊！」隨即投降般高舉雙臂，然後癱軟在沙發上不再動彈。「格勒果！你……」妹妹喊道，她握緊拳頭，惡狠狠地瞪著他。自從他變形之後，這是妹妹第一次直接跟他說的話。她跑到隔壁房間，想找些香油或任何東西來救醒昏厥的母親。格勒果也很想幫忙——要搶救照片不必急在這一時——可是他很快就黏在玻璃上了，要很用力才能掙脫。然後他跟著妹妹跑到隔壁房間，彷彿還能像以前那樣給她建議似的，卻只能呆愣在她身後，看著她在瓶瓶罐罐中翻找，她一轉過身就赫然看到他。同時有罐瓶子落地碎了開來，一塊玻璃碎片飛濺割傷了格勒果的臉，腐蝕性的藥水濺到他身上幾滴。葛蕾特一刻也沒有耽擱，立刻捧著一大堆瓶子，跑回母親身邊，

用腳砰的一聲關上門。格勒果就這樣與母親隔離了，多虧了他，母親現在可能命在旦夕。他不敢開門，也不再像剛剛那樣想要趕走妹妹，因為她必須陪著母親。他只能在門外等著，擔憂得無以復加地責備自己。他開始到處爬行，牆壁、家具、天花板，什麼地方都爬，在絕望之中，他覺得整個房間似乎在他四周旋轉，然後就墜落在大桌子的中央。

過了些時間，格勒果仍虛弱地躺在那裡，四周寂靜無聲，也許這是個好徵兆。然後，門鈴響了，女傭當然關在廚房裡，葛蕾特必須去開門。是父親回來了。

父親從葛蕾特的神情就知道事情不對勁，他劈頭就問：「怎麼了？」

「媽昏倒了，但她現在好多了。格勒果跑出來了。」葛蕾特的聲音聽起來含糊不清，顯然她正埋在父親的懷裡說話。

「我就知道會這樣。」父親說，「我之前就告訴過妳們了，妳們女人就是不聽我的話。」

格勒果心裡知道，葛蕾特的說明過於簡短，使得他的父親誤會格勒果做了什麼粗暴的事情。格勒果照理應該安撫父親的怒氣，可是他沒有時間也沒有機會辯解，只能快速逃到自己的房門前，全身推向門口，好讓父親一從玄關走進來，就能看出兒子有意立刻回房，不需要費力驅趕他，只要有人幫忙把門打開，他就會馬上消失在他們的視線裡。

然而，他的父親卻沒有心情去洞悉他的用意，一踏進玄關就大叫：「啊！」既憤怒也得意地逮到他。格勒果把頭從門上縮回，抬頭看著父親。這個父親不是他想像中的模樣。

他承認自己最近太專注於攀爬天花板的新消遣，以至於沒有像以前一樣去關心家裡其他的事情，如果有什麼變化，他實在應該做好心理準備面對。儘管如此，眼前這個人真是他的父親嗎？以前每次格勒果出差時，這個人總會疲憊地深埋在床上，而在傍晚時分坐在扶手椅上，穿著晨袍歡迎格勒果回來，這時他並不會站起身，而是只舉起臂膀致意。偶爾在一年中的一、兩個星期日或重大節日時，他會和家人出去，走在格勒果和他母親之間，母親已經走得很慢了，父親走得比他們母子還慢，他會裹著舊大衣，全程拄著枴杖，小心翼翼地拖著步伐往前走，而他想要說話時，總是要停下腳步，把同行的人招集到他身邊。

但現在父親直挺挺地站在那裡，穿著筆挺的藍色制服，上面有金色銅扣，就像個銀行工友。他堅實的雙下巴突出於外套高挺的領子，濃密的眉毛下，一雙炯黑的眼睛，怒視的目光警戒且具有穿透力；他之前蓬亂的白髮往兩邊梳得光亮平整，戴著縫有金色字母的帽子，那顯然是某家銀行的標誌。他把帽子遠遠地往房間那頭的沙發擲去，再用手拂開外套下襬，雙手插進褲袋裡，帶著嚴峻的表情走向格勒果。

好像連他自己也不知道要怎麼辦才好，無論如何，他不尋常地把腳抬高，巨大的靴子底部使格勒果嚇呆了。無論如何，格勒果沒有愣住太久，因為自從新生活的第一天開始，他便明白父親只相信嚴厲的方式才能制服他。

於是他趕緊逃離父親，當父親站著不動時他也停下，每當父親稍微輕輕一動，他就驚惶得趕緊逃跑。他們就這樣在房間裡繞了幾圈，沒有分出任何勝負，事實上速度緩慢得根本不像是在追逐。格勒果一直沒有離開地板，因為他擔心飛上牆壁或天花板的舉動，會讓父親將這種行徑視為有攻擊惡意。但無論如何，他也無法繼續這麼兜圈子，因為父親每走一步，他就必須要前進好幾步。他已經開始喘不過氣來了，他的肺在前半段的生活中本來就不太可靠。

為了集中所有精神地逃跑，很難睜開眼睛，以至於他步伐蹣跚。惶然之中，除了一味地往前衝，他完全想不到其他任何方法。他忘了自己可以隨意爬上牆壁，可是這個房間擺了許多雕工精良、外型尖刺銳利的家具，把牆壁都擋住了。突然之間，有什麼東西無意間飛過，掉落在他身邊後滾到他面前。原來是一顆蘋果，緊接著飛來了第二顆蘋果，格勒果嚇得停下腳步，現在就算飛起來也沒有用了。因為父親已下

定決心要連番襲擊他了。

父親的口袋裝滿了從餐櫥的盆子取來的水果，也不費神瞄準，就把蘋果一顆顆地砸向他。紅色的小蘋果好像通了電般，在地板上滾動、互相碰撞。有一顆蘋果擦過格勒果的背部，因為力道不大所以彈了開來，沒有對他造成傷害，但是馬上就又飛來另外一顆，直接命中他的背部並陷了進去。

格勒果硬拖著身體想要往前走，以為這樣就可以讓料想不到的劇痛消失，可是他彷彿被釘子釘在那裡，只得平躺下來，所有感覺都已經錯亂了。他最後看到自己的房門被扯開，母親衝了出來，妹妹則跟在後面尖叫。母親只穿著襯衣，因為妹妹為了讓她緩過氣來，已經把她的外衣都解開。格勒果看到母親跑到父親那裡，鬆脫的襯裙一件又一件地掉在地上，她步履艱難地跨過，直撲進父親的懷裡，緊緊抱著他——格勒果的視線只能看到這裡——而其實她的手繞過丈夫的頸子，為兒子求饒。

第 3 章

　　格勒果重傷後過了一個多月。那顆蘋果仍嵌在他的身軀上，沒有人敢冒險幫他去除，那顆蘋果成了警惕。雖然變成了目前既悲慘又討人厭的模樣，但蘋果提醒著父親，格勒果仍是家庭的一分子，不應該當敵人對待。既然是家人，就有克制厭惡感的義務，除了容忍，還是容忍。

　　他身上的傷勢使他變得不良於行，也許再也復原不了了。現在要爬過房間，他得花上很久很久的時間，就像個年老的傷兵，要爬上牆壁更是不用想了。然而，依他的想法，雖然情況惡化，但現在每到傍晚時分，客廳的門就會打開。他通常早在一、兩個小時之前就會凝視著門口，門開了以後，他就會躺在黑暗的房間裡，家人看不見他，但他可以看見他們全坐在點著燈的桌邊，傾聽著他們談話，看來這是家人一致同意的額外補償。令他感到欣慰滿足，因為和他之前的竊聽大不相同。

　　當然，他們的交談沒有以前那般生氣勃勃。以往出差在

外，下榻於旅館，筋疲力竭地鑽進潮濕的被窩時，經常會想念起家人交談的光景。他們現在多半是沉默不語。晚餐過後，父親會在扶手椅上打瞌睡，母親和妹妹則在死寂中聊著天，但仍提防著。母親彎身傾向燈光，為一家時髦服飾店縫製高級內襯衣物。妹妹已經受聘為店員了，夜晚自修速記和法語，希望之後能獲得更好的工作職位。有時候父親會醒過來，好像不曉得自己曾經睡著，對母親說：「妳今天縫了好久！」然後又立即睡去，母親和妹妹兩人只好無奈地彼此面對面，相視而笑。

父親的脾氣執拗，堅持在家裡也要穿著制服，讓晨袍無用地掛在衣架上，他穿戴整齊坐著睡覺，好像在家裡也在等候上司的叫喚，可隨時執行勤務般。如此一來，即便母親和妹妹悉心保護，他那原先就不是全新的制服開始顯得汙穢不堪。格勒果經常整夜望著那有許多油膩汙漬的制服，金色的銅扣卻總是擦得亮晶晶的。老人家穿著這身衣服坐著睡覺，雖然極不舒服，卻也睡得相當安穩。

等到鐘響十下，母親就會輕聲喚醒父親，要他上床睡覺，畢竟在客廳並不能真的好眠，而他六點就要上班，良好的睡眠是他最需要的。可是從父親成為銀行工友後，就有了那個牛脾氣，總是堅持要在桌邊多待一會兒，雖然他還是會再打起瞌睡，最後非得好說歹說，他才願意從扶手椅換到床上。即便母親和妹妹花上一刻鐘的時間，對他婉言相勸，父親仍是搖晃著腦袋，閉著眼睛拒絕起身。這時母親就會去拉他的袖子，在他耳邊說盡好話，妹妹也要丟下功課，過去幫母親的忙，但父親還是不肯就範。他會在椅子上陷得更深，除非兩個女人從他的腋下把他撐起來，他才會張開眼睛，交替看著她們倆。這時他通常會說上這句話：「這就是人生。這就是我安詳、平靜的晚年。」在妻女的支撐下，他會掙扎著站起來，彷彿自己是個重大的負荷，麻煩她們把他送到房門口之後，他才會揮揮手甩開她們，自己進房去，但母親仍會放下縫紉器具，妹妹擱下筆，跟在父親後面，進去照顧他上床。

　　家人操勞過度，疲憊不堪，誰還有時間關心格勒果飲食之外的事情呢？家計一天比一天窘迫，已經請女傭離開了。但每天早晚都會有一個滿頭白髮、骨架寬大的清潔女傭來做些粗活，其他工作則都是格勒果的母親在做，她還要縫一大堆衣物。連以前母親和妹妹自豪地戴去參加宴會和慶典的各種家傳首飾也賣掉了。有天晚上他們在討論換取了多少錢時，格勒果才知道這件事。而就他們目前的處境來說，最煩心的其實就是無法搬離這間過於寬敞的公寓，何況家人也不知道要如何搬動格勒果。不過格勒果清楚知道，不能搬家的主要因素並不是考慮到他，因為只要準備一個大小適當的箱子，上面挖些氣孔，就可以輕易搬動他了。真正阻擾他們搬家的原因，是深陷於澈底的絕望與悲傷不幸的自憐，因為他們的親友都不曾遭遇過這樣的事。

世間對窮人的磨難，他們全都經歷了。父親為銀行的小職員送早餐，母親花費心力為陌生人縫製內衣，妹妹在櫃臺後面對顧客唯命是從。除此之外，家人已經無力去顧及其他的事了。

母親和妹妹送父親就寢後回到客廳，她們放著工作，緊緊相依坐著。母親這時會指著格勒果的房門說：「葛蕾特，去把那扇門關上。」他又再度留在黑暗之中。而門外的女人臉上交織著淚水，或可能已哭乾了雙眼，只是默默盯著桌面。這時，格勒果背上的傷又疼了起來。

格勒果幾乎早晚都睡不著覺。他經常有個念頭，就是下一次房門打開時，他會和以前一樣，把家計重擔一手攬下來。不僅如此，經過這麼久的時間，他的腦海裡有時會出現老闆、經理、學徒、愚蠢至極的看門人，還有別家公司的兩三個朋友，某個會勾起他甜美回憶的女清潔員，那是在一間鄉下的旅館；還有一個在帽飾店工作，他非常愛慕卻遲遲沒有表白的女收銀員……連同那些他不認識的人或早已淡忘的人都一一浮現。這些人不僅沒有來幫助他和家人，還從此敬而遠之，格勒果也很開心他們從他的生命中消失。

然而格勒果沒有心思去擔心家人，因為他正為家人疏於照料他的需求而滿懷怒氣。雖然他自己也不曉得想要吃些什麼，肚子也不餓，卻計畫著如何潛入廚房，找一些合他口味的食物。妹妹不再花心思帶他可能會喜歡吃的食物，不過會在早上和中午趕去上班之前，用腳將食物很快地踢進他的房間，不管格勒果多半只是嚐了一口，或是連碰都沒碰，她都會在傍晚時用掃帚一次掃出去。現在晚間的清理工作，她已經做得草率到不能再更草率了。

牆面上拖著一條條很是骯髒的痕跡，到處都是成堆的灰塵和汙物。起初格勒果會在妹妹進來時，故意待在特別髒的角落，藉這個方式來表達不滿。可是就算他在那裡坐上幾個星期，也無法改變她的態度。她和格勒果一樣看得到那些髒汙，但是她打定主意不去理會。而且，她變得敏感、容易發怒，架勢凌駕於全家上，她時時注意著那些髒汙是不是都還在，霸道地認為只有她有資格清理格勒果的房間。

母親有一次把格勒果的房間大掃除了一番，她還用了幾桶水才終於完成清掃。結果房間散不去的濕氣，讓格勒果很不高興，他懶洋洋地，悶悶不樂地躺在沙發上，動也不動。沒多久，母親便因為打掃了他的房間而受罪。那天晚上，妹妹一發現格勒果房間的變化，便氣憤得跑到客廳，不管母親舉起雙手哀求，就號哭了起來。父親此時當然從扶手椅上驚醒了，她的父母先是在一旁無奈地看著，接著變得氣憤難耐。父親先是責備右邊的母親沒有把清掃房間的工作留給葛蕾特；接著又大聲地對左邊的妹妹叫嚷，說以後再也不讓她去清掃格勒果的房間了；母親則想要把激動得失控的父親拉進寢室；妹妹哭得渾身顫抖，小巧的拳頭捶打著桌面；格勒果氣得嘶聲大叫，因爲他們沒有一個人想到把門關上，以免讓他目睹這場紛爭。

　　儘管現在妹妹已經因爲工作而疲倦不堪，相比之前，也開始對照顧格勒果的事感到厭煩。即便如此，母親爲了她，也依然不會再進入格勒果房間。不過格勒果並沒有因此被忽視，因爲現在有那位老女傭。這個老寡婦健壯的身軀，肯定幫她度過了長年的辛勞，而她一點也不怕格勒果。她有一次偶然打開他的房門，完全不是因爲好奇，但她瞥見了格勒果。格勒果被她嚇了一跳後四處奔跑，即便根本沒有人追著他跑，老婦人只是雙手抱胸站在那裡盯著他。從此之後，她早晚都會偷偷打開一道門縫，看看他的情況。起初她還會用一些她自認爲親切的話語叫他過來，譬如：「過來一下，你這隻老糞金龜！」或「唷！那邊的老糞金龜！」格勒果不會回應無禮的舉動，他繼續待在原地不動，好像那扇門從未開啓過。

　　與其容許老太婆興致一來就百無聊賴地打擾他，不如命令她每天來打掃他的房間，這粗魯的老太婆！有一天一大早，大雨正在敲擊窗沿，大概是春天到來的徵兆，老太婆又來囉嗦了，格勒果被攪弄得發火，就往她那裡跑去，好像要攻擊她，不過速度緩慢且無殺傷力。老太婆並沒有因此感到畏懼，只是舉起了正好在門邊的椅子。她瞠目結舌地站在那裡，唯有把椅子丟到格勒果的背上，她的表情才會回復。看到格勒果轉過身去，她一面鎮定地把椅子放回角落，一面說道：「你不可以再這麼做了！」

格勒果現在幾乎都不吃東西了。他只有在正好經過食物時，才會好玩地吃一口含在嘴裡，通常過了一個小時就會把它都吐出來。剛開始他以為是房間的改變使他懊惱，他才會吃不下東西，可是他很快就適應了房間種種的改變。家人已經養成習慣，把沒有地方擺的東西都堆進他的房間，而現在這些東西多得很，因為家裡有個房間租給了三個房客。這三名嚴肅的男士都有滿臉的鬍鬚，有次格勒果透過門縫看到過。他們對整潔的要求一絲不苟，不僅是他們的房間，既然同住在這間公寓裡，他們對所有的擺設都很挑剔，尤其是廚房。它們就是無法忍受毫無用處且粗製劣造的東西。

他們甚至把自己需要的家具給帶來了，因此很多東西都變得多餘，但又是些無法售出，也難以捨棄的東西。所有雜物都堆進了格勒果的房間，連煤灰箱和廚房的垃圾桶也來了。暫時不需要的東西都由老太婆丟到格勒果的房裡，而老太婆不管做什麼事都很匆促，幸好格勒果通常只會看到堆進來的物品，還有她伸過來的手。也許她是想等到有機會時再把東西拿走，或是先堆積起來再一起拿去丟，但事實上，那些東西就一直放在她丟下的地方，除非格勒果在經過時把它

推開。最初他因為沒有足夠的空間爬行了，所以被迫這麼做，但後來逐漸發現移動東西很有趣，只是在這種活動過後便累得要死，發現自己是如此不幸，動也不動地躺上好幾個小時。

由於房客經常會在公共的客廳享用晚餐，客廳的門有好幾晚都關著，但是格勒果泰然接受。因為有時候傍晚門打開了，他也沒有興致，只是躺在家人看不到的黑暗角落裡伸展筋骨。可是有一次，老太婆沒有把門完全關上，晚上房客進來吃飯時把燈點亮了，這時房門還留著一道縫沒有關上。他們坐在桌子的上位，那是以前格勒果和父母親吃飯時坐的地方。他們攤開餐巾，拿起刀叉。母親立刻端著一盤肉走了進來，妹妹則緊跟在後面，拿著一盤堆積如山的馬鈴薯。食物冒出熱騰騰的蒸氣，房客俯身看著眼前的食物，彷彿在開動之前要先檢驗一番似的，中間那位紳士似乎比其他兩人更有話語權，他切下了一塊肉放在盤子上，顯然是要確認是否煮得夠嫩，不然就要送回廚房。他看起來挺滿意，原本在一旁屏息看著的母親和妹妹，這才鬆了一口氣，露出笑容。

格勒果的家人現在都是在廚房用餐。儘管如此，父親在進廚房之前總要先到客廳來，手裡拿著帽子，深深地鞠個躬，在桌邊繞上一圈。房客此時會站起身來，藏在鬍鬚中的嘴低聲嘀咕了幾句。父親離開後，便獨留他們自己吃飯，幾乎沒有人開口說話。格勒果覺得很奇怪，他總是能夠從桌邊傳來的各種聲響中分辨出牙齒的咀嚼聲，那好像在告訴他，有牙齒才能吃東西，就算擁有最俊俏的下巴，沒有牙齒也無用武之地。

「我很餓了，」格勒果自言自語著，「可是那種東西我才不要吃。爲什麼房客能坐享一頓餐，我卻要在這裡餓肚子！」

就在那天晚上，廚房傳來了小提琴的聲音──打從變形之後，格勒果就不記得聽過小提琴聲了。房客這時已經吃完晚餐，中間那個人拿出報紙，各分一張給其他兩人，現在他們正慵懶地靠在椅背上，一邊抽菸一邊看報。小提琴聲一響，他們就豎起耳朵，站起身，踮著腳尖走到玄關口，三個人緊貼在那裡聽著。

廚房的人大概聽到了他們走動的聲音。「小提琴的聲音是不是吵到你們了，先生？我可以叫她馬上停止。」父親喊道。

「怎麼會，」中間的房客說：「可否請撒摩札小姐出來，在我們這裡拉琴？這個房間比較方便，也舒服多了。」

「那太好了，謝謝。」父親叫道，好像他就是拉琴的人。

房客便走回客廳等待。不久，父親搬著譜架，母親帶著樂譜，妹妹則拿著小提琴進來。妹妹平靜地準備演奏。父母從來沒有當過房東，因而對房客太過於謙恭，竟不敢坐在自己的椅子上。父親靠在門邊，制服外套扣得很整齊，他的右手就插在兩個鈕扣之間。有個房客讓了一把椅子給母親坐，她沒有移動那人隨手擺放的椅子，而是在一邊的角落坐了下來。

妹妹開始演奏了，父親和母親在兩邊專注地看著女兒雙手的動作。格勒果被琴聲所吸引，大膽地稍微往前移動，他的頭已經進到客廳裡面了。他一點都不驚訝自己越來越不在意他人，有段時間，為他人設想總是他引以為傲的優點。但此時此刻，他應該像以往那樣體貼，將自己藏匿起來。他的房間已經積了厚厚一層灰，稍一走動就會揚起塵埃，使他全身都是灰塵，絨毛、頭髮和食物殘渣也同樣附著在他的背上和身上。他已經對任何事情都滿不在乎，當然也不會翻轉過身，在地毯上把自己擦乾淨──原本他一天都會這樣做上幾次，清潔自己。如今這付德性，他也不避諱再往前挪一點點，進入一塵不染的客廳地板。

這時，還沒有人注意到他。家人也都被琴聲給深深吸引，但是房客似乎不是如此。紳士們的手都插在褲袋裡，站在譜架後面，近得可以看到樂譜──必然會妨礙妹妹拉琴──他們很快地退到窗邊，低著頭輕聲說話。父親不安地觀察著他們的舉動，他們那副樣子是再明顯不過了。他們原

先以為可以聽到動人愉悅的演奏，結果卻感到很失望。他們已經聽夠了演奏，只是出於禮貌才會忍受自己的平靜被侵擾。從他們三人不斷地抽著雪茄，吞雲吐霧的樣子，就可以知道他們感到煩躁。然而，妹妹拉出來的琴聲是這麼地優美，她的臉靠在一邊，眼睛哀傷而專注地追逐著音符。

格勒果又往前爬了一點點，把頭伏在地上，希望有可能與她的視線交接。如果他是動物，音樂怎麼會使他如此陶醉呢？他覺得眼前似乎敞開了一條路，通往他所渴望的精神糧食。他決定勇往直前，走到妹妹那裡，銜住她的裙子，希望拉她進去他的房間裡演奏小提琴，因為這裡沒有一個人如他一般欣賞她的表演。他不會再讓妹妹離開自己的房間，至少在他有生之年絕不容許。他可怕的外表將首次派上用場，他要同時看緊每一扇門，對入侵者嘶吼嚇退他們。不過妹妹是不能強迫的，她應該要自願和他在一起，與他並坐在沙發上，對他垂下耳朵，聽他吐露說，他以前曾下定決心要送她去唸音樂學校，如果不是遭逢不幸，去年耶誕夜──耶誕節是否真的過了呢？──他就會向大家宣布，不管有沒有人反對。聽了這番傾訴，妹妹會感動得流下淚來，格勒果就會把身體挺到她的肩膀，親吻她的頸子。自從她開始上班後，已不在脖子那裡配戴緞帶或領子了。

「撒摩札先生！」中間的房客對格勒果的父親大叫，不再多發一語地，指著正在慢慢往前爬的格勒果。小提琴聲頓時停住了，中間的房客先是對他的朋友搖搖頭，然後回頭盯著格勒果後又搖搖頭。父親並沒有去驅趕格勒果，他似乎認為安撫房客比較重要，儘管他們並沒有驚慌，而且顯然覺得格勒果比小提琴演奏還有趣。

　　父親趕緊走向他們，張開手臂，敦請他們回房，同時也擋住他們的視線，以自己的體態阻擾他們看到格勒果。房客們開始有點氣惱，沒準是因為老人家的舉動，還是因為一直以來都有像格勒果這樣的鄰居與他們同住，他們卻被蒙在鼓裡。他們要求父親解釋，對他揮動手臂表達不滿，也不安地捻著鬍子，然後心不甘情不願地緩慢退回房間裡。妹妹站在原地，彷彿在為演奏突然被打斷而不知所措，她拿著小提琴和琴弓的手無力地下垂著，彷彿仍在演奏般雙眼還盯著樂譜。突然之間，她恢復神智振作起來，把小提琴往椅子上那氣喘吁吁，難以平復的母親膝上扔去，就跑進隔壁房間。三名房客因為父親的引導，已經快走到房門了。在妹妹熟練的動作下，床上的枕頭和被褥被高高地掀起、鋪整，一轉眼就準備就緒，房客還未踏進房門，她就已經鋪好床，迅速地溜了出去。

　　老人似乎又一次讓自己的牛脾氣牽著走，把什麼都拋在腦後，忘了每回都會向房客致意。只顧著把他們趕進房間，結果到了房門口，中間的房客用力跺腳，才令父親停住腳步。

第 3 章

「我要向你宣告，」房客說，舉起一隻手，同時看著格勒果的母親和妹妹。「由於這間屋裡的家庭狀況令人厭惡，」他往地板上痛快地啐了一口，「我現在就要解除租約，當然這些日子的房租我一毛也不會付，相反地，我還考慮向你要求賠償，證據很容易取得，別以為我在開玩笑。」說完，他直視前方，彷彿在等待著什麼。果然，他兩個朋友立即表達了各自的立場：「我們也要解約。」隨後中間那個人就抓住門把，啪嗒一聲把門關上。

父親搖頭晃腦地蹣跚前行，摸索著路然後跌坐在椅子上，看起來像平時傍晚準備打瞌睡那樣伸展四肢，不過他頻頻垂下頭的模樣，在那無力地晃著，根本無法入睡。自從被房客發現後，格勒果一直很安靜地待在原處。他很失望計畫沒有實現，也或許是因為過度飢餓而虛弱得無法移動。他擔憂隨時將會有一場大災難爆發，於是他躺在那裡等待著。母親的指尖顫抖得抓不住小提琴，從她的膝上掉落到地上，就連如此清亮的聲響，也沒有嚇著他。

「我親愛的父母親，」妹妹敲著桌子發出聲響作為引子，「不能再這樣下去了。也許你們還不明白，可是我非常清楚，我不會在這個怪物面前提起哥哥的名字。我的意思是：我們一定要擺脫牠。我們一直很有人性地盡力照顧牠、忍受牠，我相信沒有人會責怪我們。」

「她說得對極了。」父親自言自語著。母親仍然氣喘吁吁，突然一手摀起嘴激動地乾咳起來，眼神焦躁不安。

妹妹跑到母親身邊，攙扶著她。父親似乎不再對葛蕾特的話感到疑惑，他端坐起身，手指撫弄著他那頂帽子，帽子就放在還未收拾的碗盤之間，並且不時回頭去看一動也不動的格勒果。

「我們一定要設法擺脫牠，」妹妹這次斬釘截鐵地對父親說道，母親則因為咳得太厲害了，聽不進任何話。「不然你們會被殺死，我看得很清楚。我們工作已經夠辛苦了，我們三人都是，回到家還要忍受無止境的折磨。至少我是不能再忍受了。」說完，她放聲大哭，淚水滴在母親的臉上，母親下意識地用手拭去。

「女兒啊，」老人憐愛地說著，感慨地說道，「我們該怎麼做呢？」

儘管果斷地下了決定，邊哭泣邊聳肩的妹妹，則是一臉茫然。

「如果他聽得懂我們的話就好了。」父親說，半帶詢問的口氣。葛蕾特邊哭邊猛烈地揮著手，表示那是不可能的。

「如果他聽得懂我們的話就好了，」父親重覆道，閉上眼睛思量著女兒斷定不可能的想法。「也許我們可以跟他講個明白。不過看這個樣子……」

「他一定要離開，」妹妹說，「這是唯一的辦法，爸爸。你一定停止認爲他是格勒果。我們一直把他當格勒果看待，這才是我們悲慘的原因。可是，他怎麼會是格勒果？如果他是格勒果，他早該想到人類不能和這種怪物一起生活，而自行離開了。那麼我們雖然失去了哥哥，但我們會懷念著與他共度的美好回憶活下去。可是現在，這個怪物會迫害我們，嚇走房客，顯然想要自己獨占整間公寓，使我們全部都露宿街頭。看呀，爸爸！」她突然大叫，「他又來了！」

格勒果無法理解她爲何會這麼驚慌，她甚至拋下母親，把椅子推開，好像寧可犧牲母親也不要靠近格勒果。她逃到父親後面，父親也站起身，只因爲她的倉皇舉動而生起氣來，他舉起臂膀保護她。

然而，格勒果一點都沒有要對誰不利的意思，尤其是對他的妹妹。他只不過要掉轉方向，以便爬回房間，可是他的動作看起來令人驚駭，因爲身軀孱弱，只有不斷抬起頭，再抵著地板上推動，才能艱難地轉身。他停頓一會兒看了看四周，大家似乎看出了他的善意，剛剛的驚嚇已不再。現在誰都不說話，只是悲哀地默默看著他。母親躺在椅子上，雙腳合併，僵硬地直伸出去，眼睛因爲虛弱而快閉起來了。父親和妹妹肩並肩坐著，妹妹的手臂圍在父親的脖頸上。

也許我可以繼續掉轉方向，格勒果心想，又開始行動。但是相當吃力，他無法避免喘息，必須不時停下來喘口氣。

　　沒有人過來干擾他，任由他自己慢慢來。他換好了方向，立刻開始爬回去。此處與房門的距離令他驚訝，他想不明白自己如此虛弱，剛剛是何以迅速走了這麼遠的，他一點都沒察覺自己移動了這麼多步。他一心只想爬快一點，沒有注意到家人連一句話或一聲嘆息也沒有。

　　到了房門口，他才轉過頭來，但因為頸項僵硬，他無法完全轉過頭來，不過他看到後面依然毫無動靜，只有妹妹站了起來。最後他瞥向母親，她已經完全睡著了。他整個身體才剛進入房間，門就被倏地關上，扣上鐵閂，上了鎖。

　　這一連串的聲響嚇著了格勒果，他細小的腳都捲縮了起來。是妹妹迅速地鎖上房門的，她早就站起身來等著，在剎時之間衝過去，格勒果並沒有聽見她過來，就聽到她一邊扭轉門鎖，一邊對父母說：「終於解決了！」

　　「現在要怎麼辦？」格勒果自言自語，在黑暗中四下張望。他很快就發現到，他一步也走不了。這一點並不令他驚訝，他反而覺得能用這些纖細的腳走路才是不自然的。無論如何，他覺得比較自在了。雖然全身都很痛，但疼痛似乎正在逐漸減輕，最後將會完全消失。背上的爛蘋果和旁邊發炎的地方都覆蓋著白色的塵埃，也早已失去知覺了。他想起溫

馨和藹的家人，因而他覺得自己必須消失，也許意圖比妹妹
還要堅決。懷著空虛而平靜的思緒，就這麼直到塔鐘敲響了
凌晨三點。他看見曙光在窗外逐漸亮起，接著他的頭不情願
地垂到地板上，吐出最後一絲微弱的氣息。

　　老太婆早上來到時，照常以其蠻力和急性子的做事方
式，砰砰砰的關上所有的房門，儘管已多少次勸告她，只要
她一進屋，還是使屋裡的人都不能好好安睡。依習慣窺探格
勒果的房間時，她並沒有發現異常。她以為格勒果是故意一
動也不動地躺著，假裝在發脾氣，也以為格勒果很會搞怪。
她正好手上拿著長柄掃把，就從門口用它來搔抓格勒果。他
沒有一點反應，她惱火了，就更用力去戳他，看到他在地板
上被往前推動卻不反抗，她才起了疑心。不久她發現怎麼回
事後，就睜大了眼睛，驚訝得吁了一聲，她沒能保持鎮定太
久，就衝去拉開主人的臥房，朝昏暗的房內大聲叫喊：「你
們來看，他死了，躺在那裡死翹翹了！」

　　撒摩札夫婦倆從雙人床上彈起身來，得先平復受到的驚
嚇，才意識到老太婆說的話。他們立刻分別從兩側下床，撒
摩札先生在肩膀上披了件毛毯，撒摩札太太只穿著睡衣，他
們直接走進格勒果的房間。這時，客廳的門也打開了，自從
來了房客，葛蕾特就在那裡睡覺。她的衣服已經穿得很整
齊，好像整晚都沒有睡覺，從她蒼白的臉龐也可以證實這一
點。

「死了？」撒摩札太太說，疑惑地望著老太婆，雖然她可以自己去確認，但事實已經清楚得無需再確認。

「應該是的。」老太婆說，為了證實，她用掃帚柄把格勒果的屍骸遠遠推到一邊。撒摩札太太遲疑著，彷彿想要阻止她，卻沒有開口。

「那麼，」撒摩札先生說，「感謝上帝。」他在胸前畫了個十字，其他三個女人也跟著他這麼做。

「你們看，他好瘦。他好久沒有吃東西了，送進來的食物幾乎都原封不動地拿出去。」葛蕾特說著，視線始終沒有離開那個屍骸。

格勒果的身軀確實變得又乾又扁，而且顯然那些腳將無法再抬起，他們沒什麼好怕的，所以才敢仔細瞧他。

「葛蕾特，和我們一起進來一下。」撒摩札太太浮起悲愴的笑容說。葛蕾特跟著父母走進他們的臥房，沒有再回頭看屍骸一眼。老太婆關上門，把窗戶完全打開。雖然還是清晨，新鮮的空氣中已經帶著些許暖意，畢竟現在已經是三月底了。

三名房客從他們的房間走出來，驚訝地發現桌上沒有備好的早餐等著他們。他們已經被忘得一乾二淨了。

「我們的早餐呢？」中間的房客不高興地問老太婆。她把手指豎在嘴上，不發一語，迅速地指向格勒果的房間。他們走了進去，房間一如以往，此時已很明亮，他們手插在有點寒酸的外套口袋裡，圍著格勒果的屍骸站著看。

撒摩札夫婦的房門終於開了，撒摩札先生穿著制服出現，一隻手摟著妻子，另一隻手摟著女兒。他們臉上都有些淚痕，葛蕾特還不時將臉壓在父親的手臂上。

「請你們立刻離開我的房子！」撒摩札先生說著，指著大門，仍然擁著兩個女人。

「你是什麼意思？」中間的房客說，露出錯愕但卑微的笑容。其他兩人把手背在後面，不停地揉搓，好像滿心歡喜地期待一場最終將由他們獲勝的爭論。

「就是我剛剛說的意思。」撒摩札先生回答，和兩個家人排成一列，一同朝那個房客走去。那人起初靜靜站著凝視著地板，彷彿正在重新梳理腦中的思緒。

「那麼我們就走吧。」他說著，抬起頭看著撒摩札先生，彷彿認為只要改成謙卑的態度，便能讓對方回心轉意。但撒摩札先生只是反覆點頭，眼神堅定。

見事態如此，這房客便邁開大步走向玄關，兩個一直在傾聽的朋友早就停止搓手，急忙機靈地隨後跟上，好像在害

怕撒摩札先生會擋在玄關，把他們和領頭拆散。三人到了玄
關，從衣架取下帽子，從置物架抽出手杖，默默行了個禮就
離開了。

　　撒摩札先生和兩個女人懷疑地跟著他們走到樓梯平台，
但是這種疑心馬上就證實是多餘的。他們倚在欄杆上，看著
三個人影緩慢但步伐平穩地走下長長的階梯，在每一層的轉
角上消失蹤影，然後在下一刻又現身。他們的影子變得越
小，撒摩札一家人對他們的興趣就越淡。一個肉店夥計遇到
他們，洋洋自得地把一個托盤頂在頭上，經過他們爬上樓。
撒摩札先生和兩個女人隨即離開平台，走回公寓，好像重擔
已經解除了。

　　他們決定休息一天，出去散個步。他們不僅值得放一天
假，也非常需要這麼做。於是他們坐在桌邊，寫三份請假
函：撒摩札先生寫給主管，撒摩札太太寫給客戶，葛蕾特則
寫給店老闆。正在寫的時候，老太婆進來通報她要走了，因
為早上的工作做完了。他們起初只是點點頭，沒有抬起頭
來，但是她一直杵在那裡，於是他們憤然看著她。

　　「什麼事？」撒摩札先生問道。

　　老太婆在門口露齒而笑，一副有好消息要告訴這家人，
但除非有人問她，否則她一句話也不說。小小的鴕鳥羽毛直
挺挺地插在她的帽子上，前後左右地飄晃著，自從她來到這

裡工作，撒摩札先生一看到那個東西就生氣。

「到底有什麼事？」撒摩札太太問道，她是老太婆較敬重的人。

「唔……」老太婆說著，熱絡地咯咯笑了起來，以至於無法馬上接著說。「你們不用煩惱要怎麼處置隔壁房間裡的東西，我都處理好了。」

撒摩札太太和葛蕾特又低下頭想繼續寫信。撒摩札先生意識到老太婆想要描述整個細節，就斷然舉起手臂阻止她。既然沒有人准許老太婆說明過程，她便想起來自己要趕時間，便惱怒地大喊：「再見，各位！」然後憤怒地轉過身去，臨走時把門甩上，發出駭人的聲響。

「今天晚上就叫她滾蛋！」撒摩札先生說，可是他的妻子和女兒都沒有回應，她們好不容易平靜下來的心似乎又被老太婆給攪亂了。她們站起身，走到窗邊，互相摟著彼此。撒摩札先生轉過身，默默注視著她們。

接著他出聲叫喚：「到這裡來吧，過去的事就讓它過去。妳們多少也該為我想一想。」兩人立刻奔到他身邊，親吻安慰他，然後很快就把信寫好。

接著他們三人一起離開了公寓，這是好幾個月以來的第一次。他們搭火車去城外的郊區。只有他們三個人的車廂

裡，洋溢著溫暖的陽光。他們舒服地靠在椅背上商量未來的
計畫，仔細盤算過後，發現三人都有工作的情況似乎還不
差。他們之前都不曾討論過三人的工作，這三份工作都很
好，也很有前途。改善處境最快的方法當然是搬家了，他們
要去租一間比格勒果選的公寓還要小、還要便宜，地點較佳
也比較實用的公寓。愉悅地談話的當下，撒摩札夫婦幾乎同
時注意到女兒越來越有生氣，雖然最近受了那麼多苦難，使
她的臉頰變得很蒼白，但是她已經變成了個身材曼妙的漂亮
女孩。他們的話越來越少，而且不自覺地交換眼神，一致同
意該是為她找個好夫婿的時候了。到了目的地，彷彿在回應
他們的新期望和美意似的，他們的女兒首先站了起來，伸展
她那青春的軀體。

飢餓
藝術家

這幾十年來，民眾對飢餓表演的興趣大減，以前舉辦這種大型表演的收入是很可觀的，可是到了現在，那已經不太可能了。我們活在不一樣的時代。有一段時期，全鎮都對飢餓藝術家充滿興趣，他餓越久，民眾對他越感興趣，每個人每天至少都要來看他一次。臨近表演後期，有些人會購買季票，從早到晚都坐在他小小的鐵籠子前面。即使是夜間也有參觀時間，會有火把來增強整體的氣氛。

　　天氣好的時候，籠子會設置在露天的地方，特地讓小孩前去觀賞飢餓藝術家。對孩子的父母來說，他只是個流行的娛樂對象，為了安全起見，將牽著孩子的手一起看。小孩會張大嘴，驚奇地看著他。飢餓藝術家臉色蒼白，穿著黑色的緊身衣，突起的肋骨非常明顯，摒棄世俗的椅子，只是墊著乾草坐在地上，有時會禮貌地點點頭，勉強擺出笑容回答問題，有時則把手伸出欄杆，讓觀眾看看他的手是多麼瘦削，然後又陷入沉思，毫不理會任何人或任何事。時鐘是籠子裡唯一的擺設，他連最重要的時鐘敲響的聲音都充耳不聞，只

是眼睛稍微張開凝視著前方，偶爾從一個小杯子啜飲少許的水，潤一潤嘴唇。

除了來來去去的一般觀衆，還有一些由民衆推選出來的人員輪流監視。很奇怪，這些人通常是屠夫，負責日夜看守飢餓藝術家，三個人一班，以防止他私下偷偷進食。這只是個形式，藉以取信大衆，因爲圈內人都知道，藝術家在絕食期間，不論在任何情況下，即使是遭到暴力脅迫，也不會吃下一丁點食物，因爲他爲藝術犧牲的榮譽感禁止他這麼做。當然，並不是每個看守人都了解這一點，常常會有些夜班的看守員在執行任務時顯得很鬆懈，故意聚在隱蔽的角落專心打牌，顯然是要給飢餓藝術家有機會吃東西，他們總以爲，飢餓藝術家會從某個祕密的地方取出食物。沒有比這種看守員更讓藝術家生氣的了：他們使他痛苦，使飢餓變得似乎難以忍受，有時候他會在這些人看守時硬撐起虛弱的身體唱歌，因爲只要他繼續唱，就能向他們證明，他們的懷疑是多麼不公平。可是一點用處也沒有，那只會令他們讚嘆他竟然能邊吃邊唱。

他最喜歡的看守員會挨著欄杆坐下，由於不滿意廳堂昏暗的光線，他們還會用演出經理發給他們的手電筒照他。他一點都不在意光線刺眼，反正他根本無法入睡，何況他隨時都能打個瞌睡，不管燈光如何，在什麼時候，即使廳堂擠滿了喧鬧的觀衆也是一樣。他很高興能夠和這種看守員共度失

眠的夜晚，也願意和他們說說笑笑，為他們講講他漂泊生涯中的故事，怎樣都好，只要能讓他保持清醒，讓他們看到，籠子裡沒有吃的東西，而他挨餓的本領比他們任何人都強。

不過他最快樂的時刻是天亮以後，他掏腰包請人給他們送來豐盛的早餐，那些人疲憊地熬了一整夜，立即以健康人旺盛的食慾狼吞虎嚥。當然有些人認為這頓早餐帶有賄賂看守員的不良企圖，可是這種說法實在是太離譜了；如果有人問他們願不願意值整晚的班，但是沒有早餐，這些人就會溜之大吉了，儘管還是不願改變對他的懷疑。

諸如此類的懷疑，是飢餓藝術家擺脫不了的。沒有人能夠日夜不停地觀看飢餓藝術家，所以沒有人可以提供第一手的證據證明他真的在嚴格持續絕食。那只有飢餓藝術家自己知道，所以他勢必是唯一對其表演感到百分之百滿意的觀眾。然而，基於其他原因，他卻從來沒有滿意過；也許他乾瘦如柴的身軀並不是絕食造成的，而是他對自己的不滿所致，使很多人出於同情心而不去看他的表演，因為這些人不忍心看他那飽受折磨的樣子。其實，只有他自己知道，絕食是如此容易，連圈內人也不曉得。這是世上最簡單的事。他並不隱瞞這一點，但是沒有人相信，頂多當他是謙虛，而大部分的人卻認為他是在做宣傳，或認為他是個騙子，飢餓對他而言當然不困難，因為他有一套技倆讓絕食變得很容易，而他竟敢厚著臉皮幾乎把真相都揭發出來。他必須忍受所有

的閒言閒語，時間一久，他也就習慣了，可是內心的不滿始終令他痛苦。每次飢餓表演期滿——這算是他的成就——他沒有一次是自動離開籠子的。

他的經理規定最長的飢餓表演期是四十天，他不能超過這個期限，即使是大都市也一樣，因為這是有根據的。根據經驗，四十天持續的廣告宣傳是能激發大眾產生興趣的最大極限，過了這段時間，市民就會開始失去興趣，捧場的觀眾會大幅減少。當然這方面會因各個城鎮或鄉村而有所不同，但是一般而言，四十天是最長的期限。

因此到了四十天，綴滿鮮花的籠子就會打開，熱心的觀眾擠滿廳堂，在軍樂隊的伴奏下，兩名醫生進到籠子裡檢測藝術家絕食後的身體，然後用擴音器宣布結果。最後會上來兩個覺得很榮幸能夠被選中的年輕女士，扶著飢餓藝術家走下通往小桌子的幾級臺階。臺階前的小桌上早已擺上精製的病人特餐。在這時候，藝術家總是會變得很頑固。當然，他還是會把已成皮包骨的手臂交給彎下身來伸手扶他的女士，卻不願意站起來。為什麼要在四十天後的這個特殊時刻結束絕食呢？他以前持續過很長的一段時間，一段無限長的時間，目前正處於最佳的飢餓狀態，或者說還不到最出色的飢餓狀態，為什麼要在現在停止呢？他原本可以餓得更久，不僅能成為有史以來的絕食記錄保持人——這一點他已經做到了——也可藉著超越人類想像的表演來打破自己保持

的記錄，因爲他覺得自己忍受飢餓的能力是無窮無盡的，爲什麼要被剝奪達到這種境界的榮譽呢？民衆假裝給他高度的讚賞，爲什麼不能對他多忍耐一下？如果他能繼續忍受飢餓，爲什麼民衆不能再繼續容忍？更何況他已經很累了，在草墊上坐著正舒服，現在卻得完全站起身，下去吃一頓安排周到卻令他反胃的餐食，只因爲有女士在場，他必須勉強忍住，而即使這麼忍著也很費力氣。他抬頭凝視女士的眼睛，她們表面上很友善，實際上卻是這麼地殘酷，他於是搖搖頭，覺得頭在虛弱的頸子上變得好沉重。

接下來，一如往常，經理走向前，一句話也沒說，因爲樂隊使他無法說話。經理把手臂舉到藝術家的頭上，好像在邀請上天俯看這個草墊上的人，這個受苦的烈士——從另一個層面來說，他的確是個烈士——再用手極爲謹愼地圈住他細瘦的腰，讓人欣賞他屛弱的情況，然後把他交給臉色蒼白的女士，同時暗中搖晃他，使他的雙腳和身體搖搖欲墜。現在藝術家任憑擺布，他的頭垂在胸前，彷彿只是碰巧停在那裡；他的身體已經變成中空，雙腳基於自我防衛的本能而緊緊夾著膝蓋，腳底卻只輕掠過地面，好像地面並不穩固，雙腳要另尋穩固的地面似的。他全身的重量儘管輕如羽毛，卻全落在其中一個女士身上，她因此氣喘吁吁，張望四周尋求求援——她沒想到這榮幸的差事會是如此難受。她起初盡量把脖子伸長，至少使她的臉不會碰到藝術家，但是她馬上就

發現那是不可能的，而比較幸運的那個同伴並不來幫她，只是以顫抖的手握著藝術家那一小把骨頭。在觀眾的鬨笑聲中，倒楣的女士哭了出來，只得由早就在那裡待命的僕人接手。

接下來要用餐了，藝術家坐在那裡，處於半昏迷的恍惚狀態，經理盡可能把一些食物塞進他的嘴裡，順口講一些玩笑話來分散觀眾對藝術家身體狀況的注意力。接下來，也許是藝術家在經理的耳邊提議的，他為觀眾乾杯，樂隊也起勁地奏樂助興，隨後觀眾逐漸散去。沒有人對這些過程感到不滿，除了飢餓藝術家自己，只有他例外，他總是不滿意。

他就這樣過了許多年，各場表演之間固定有一小段休息時間，表面上很風光，備受世人尊崇，他的心情卻是陰鬱的，而且越來越嚴重，因為沒有一個人重視他的陰鬱。他是不是需要什麼撫慰？他會不會有其他要求？如果有善

心人士憐憫他，想要給他安慰，指出他的陰鬱可能是飢餓所引起的，這時，尤其是在絕食了一段時間之後，他會以暴怒來回應，如猛獸一般搖晃籠子的欄杆，引起觀眾恐慌。但是經理有辦法處罰他的失控，也很樂於執行。他會為藝術家的行為向觀眾道歉，承認那種行為是可以原諒的，因為絕食使他易怒，這是飲食充足的人很難理解的；他話鋒一轉，接著說藝術家誇耀自己可以絕食更久，這種說法簡直就是荒謬至極；經理讚揚他在這種狀況下堅定不移地表現出勃勃的雄心、良好的意志力和偉大的克己精神，然後拿出照片，輕易地推翻藝術家的說法。照片也供出售，上面顯示藝術家在絕食的第四十天躺在床上，虛弱得奄奄一息。對於這種扭曲事實的手法，藝術家雖然很熟悉，卻每次都令他心灰意冷，無法消受。明明表演都是被迫提前收場，卻被扭曲成是他無力完成演出！要對抗這種誤解，對抗全世界的無知是不可能的。經理說話時，他通常還能虔誠地站在欄杆邊聆聽，但一看到照片出現，他就會鬆開欄杆上的手，咕噥一聲坐回草墊，安心的觀眾將會再次靠攏，圍著鐵籠觀賞他。

幾年之後，這些場景的目擊者回想起這一幕時，通常也不知道自己是怎麼一回事，因為在這段期間發生了前面提到過的大眾喜好的改變，那似乎是在一夜之間發生的，也許有更深入的原因，但是誰在乎呢？無論如何，飽受歡迎的飢餓藝術家突然發現自己被湊熱鬧的人遺棄了，那些人都撇下他

湧向其他更有趣的表演活動。最後一次經理帶著他走遍半個歐洲，想要知道這種傳統的表演是否還有市場，結果徒勞無功，好像私下約好了似的，各地區都出現明顯排斥飢餓表演的傾向。當然冰凍三尺非一日之寒，許多徵兆在巔峰時期沒有注意或加以壓制，現在想要採取什麼對策已經來不及了。飢餓表演一定會在未來的某一天再度流行，但是這並無法安慰活在當代的人。那麼，飢餓藝術家要怎麼辦呢？他在當紅的時候獲得過成千上萬人的掌聲，很難壓低身段去鄉下市集的路邊表演，而說到改行，他不僅年紀太大，也太迷戀飢餓這一行，不可能放棄。所以他告別了經理，他非凡生涯中的夥伴，接受大馬戲團的聘用；為了免於情緒波動，合約的條文他連看都沒看。

馬戲團很龐大，有無數需要更換和補充的人員、動物、器材，隨時都需要人手，連飢餓藝術家也要。當然他要求得並不多，而且他是個特例，不僅是因為藝術家本身，也因為他長年累積的名聲。確實他的表演性質很獨特，不會因為年齡增長而遜色，也不會有人說，這名藝術家已經過了巔峰時期，因此再也無法表現出最傑出的職業技能，才想在馬戲團找個安靜的角落棲身。相反地，飢餓藝術家斷然表示，他的飢餓表演和以前一樣好，這是絕對可信的。他甚至宣稱，如果他的飢餓表演能夠隨心所欲——這個要求立刻獲准——他可以創下從未有人達到的記錄，震驚全世界。這個說法當然

令其他專業人員失笑，因爲他沒有考慮到輿論的轉變，飢餓藝術家一興奮就忘了這一點。

不過，飢餓藝術家並沒有失去觀察現實的能力，心裡知道他和籠子不被當作重頭戲擺在場子中間是理所當然的，他被安置在場外，靠近獸籠，位於人群出入的要道。有個色彩鮮麗的大招牌立在籠子旁邊，說明可在籠子裡看到什麼。觀眾在中場的休息時間湧去看野獸時，都得經過飢餓藝術家的籠子，在那裡駐足片刻，要不是通道狹窄，有人在後面推擠，不明白爲什麼前面的人要停下腳步，不直接去觀看刺激的野獸，否則觀眾應該可以多待一會兒，從從容容地站著觀看。這也就是爲什麼飢餓藝術家想要躲避人群，他原先當然也很期盼這些參觀時刻，把這個時段當成生命的主要成就。起初他迫切期待中場的休息，看到群眾朝著他蜂擁而來，他就欣喜若狂，但過了不久，就算是幾近再頑固自欺也不能否認這個事實——他慢慢確定，從一群又一群湧來的觀眾中看出，毫無例外的，大部分的人都是專門來看野獸的。但是不管怎麼說，看著遠處的觀眾朝自己走來是令他最爲高興的事，他們湧向籠子時，持續不斷的叫囂聲和謾罵聲亂成一片，有些人想要停下來好好看他表演，不是眞的有興趣，只是故意跟其他人唱反調——他對這些人甚感厭惡——而另一些人則是直接去觀看野獸。

大批人群經過之後，就是一些來晚的人，雖然沒有人阻

礙他們停下來，他們卻邁著大步匆匆走過，深怕來不及觀看野獸，對飢餓藝術家連瞧都不瞧一眼。偶爾運氣好，會有個家長帶著小孩來到，指著飢餓藝術家，詳細地講解眼前景象的意義，說明在多年以前他自己也看過類似但精采許多的表演。那些懵懂無知的孩子，不管是在校內還是校外都沒有充分的準備來吸收這堂課——他們哪裡懂得飢餓？——但是從他們專注而明亮的眼睛可以看出，可能會有更美好的新時代來臨。飢餓藝術家經常自言自語著，如果籠子不是離野獸這麼近，也許情況會好一點。現在這樣很容易使觀眾選擇去看野獸，更不用說野獸的惡臭、晚上的喧鬧，還有給野獸送生肉來的聲響和餵食時間的吼叫，在在令他感到沮喪。可是他不敢向管理當局抱怨，畢竟他得感謝那些動物使一群群觀眾經過他的籠子，那裡面總有一、兩個人會對他感興趣。如果他要觀眾注意到他的存在，那麼觀眾馬上就會發現，他——確切地說——只不過是通往獸欄要道上的障礙，誰曉得他們會把他塞到哪裡去呢？

當然他只是個小小的障礙，而且會越來越小。在當今這個時代，竟然有人指望觀眾對飢餓藝術家產生興趣，大家對他已經見怪不怪了，而就是這種態度宣判了他的命運。他要餓多久就餓多久，他也真的奉行不悖，可是現在什麼都救不了他了，觀眾一個個飛快地從他面前經過。試試看跟誰說說飢餓的藝術吧！可是沒有飢餓過的人，絕對無法了解。精美

的招牌變得髒兮兮的，已經無法判讀：用來計算飢餓表演天數的小牌子，本來每天都要填上新的數字，現在已很久沒人更新紀錄了，因為幾個星期過後，連記錄員自己都覺得這件小事毫無意義。藝術家就只是像以前所夢想的那樣，日復一日地飢餓下去，而且就像他從前所預想得那般容易。可是沒有人計算天數，連藝術家自己都不計算，沒有人知道他刷新了多少記錄，他的心情越來越沉重。如果偶爾來了個閒人停下來，把牌子上的舊數字拿來逗笑取樂，說這是騙人的勾當，那這人所說的話即是冷漠和生性惡意下所造就的最愚蠢的誑語，因為飢餓藝術家並沒有欺騙，他工作得很真誠，是這個世界騙取了他的酬勞。

無論如何，又過了許多天，表演終於到了尾聲。有一天，一名管理員注意到那個籠子，就詢問服務員為什麼把一個這麼好的籠子閒置不用，裡面還鋪著爛草。沒有人知道，直到有個人看到招牌，才想起有個飢餓藝術家。他們用棍子撥弄爛草，發現他在裡面。

「你還不吃東西嗎？」管理員問他，「你到底什麼時候才要停止？」

「請各位原諒我，」飢餓藝術家以微弱的聲音訴說，只有管理員能聽見他說話，因為他把耳朵貼在欄杆上。

「當然，」管理員說，用手指敲敲前額，讓服務員了解

那個人的情況。「我們原諒你。」

「我一直希望你們能夠欣賞我的表演。」飢餓藝術家說。

「我們的確很欣賞。」管理員親切地說。

「可是你們不應該欣賞。」飢餓藝術家說。

「那我們就不欣賞。」管理員說，「為什麼我們不應該欣賞？」

「因為我絕食是不得已的。」飢餓藝術家說。

「你這個人真是不一樣，」管理員說，「為什麼你是不得已的？」

「因為，」他虛弱地說著，且稍稍抬起頭，噘起雙唇，直伸向管理員的耳朵，彷彿要親吻似的，惟恐對方漏聽了一個字。「因為我找不到合胃口的食物。如果我找得到，請你相信，我一定不會驚動他人，會像你和任何人一樣，吃得飽飽的。」

這是他臨終的話語，他渙散的眼睛流露出堅定但不再驕傲的信念：他要繼續餓下去。

「好了，把這裡清理乾淨！」管理員說。

他們把飢餓藝術家連同爛草一起埋了，然後在籠子裡關上一隻小花豹。即使是感覺最遲鈍的人看到這隻兇猛的動物在籠子裡活蹦亂跳，也會感到賞心悅目。小花豹過得很好，服務員毫不猶豫地送上牠喜歡的食物。牠甚至不眷戀失去的自由，他高貴的軀體應有盡有，什麼都不缺，似乎連自由也隨身攜帶著；自由彷彿潛藏在牠的下顎，生命的喜悅隨著猛烈的熱情從牠的喉嚨噴湧而出，令觀眾很難承受隨之而來的震撼。可是他們穩住自己，擠在籠子旁邊，絲毫不肯離去。

The
Metamorphosis

CHAPTER I

One morning, as Gregor Samsa was waking up from anxious dreams, he discovered that in bed he had been changed into a monstrous verminous bug. He lay on his armour-hard back and saw, as he lifted his head up a little, his brown, arched abdomen divided up into rigid bow-like sections. From this height the blanket, just about ready to slide off completely, could hardly stay in place.

His numerous legs, pitifully thin in comparison to the rest of his circumference, flickered helplessly before his eyes.

"What's happened to me," he thought. It was no dream.

His room, a proper room for a human being, only somewhat too small, lay quietly between the four well-known walls. Above the table, on which an unpacked collection of sample cloth goods was spread out (Samsa was a traveling salesman) hung the picture which he had cut out of an illustrated magazine a little while ago and set in a pretty gilt frame. It was a picture of a woman with a fur hat

and a fur boa. She sat erect there, lifting up in the direction of the viewer a solid fur muff into which her entire forearm disappeared.

Gregor's glance then turned to the window. The dreary weather (the rain drops were falling audibly down on the metal window ledge) made him quite melancholy. "Why don't I keep sleeping for a little while longer and forget all this foolishness," he thought. But this was entirely impractical, for he was used to sleeping on his right side, and in his present state he couldn't get himself into this position. No matter how hard he threw himself onto his right side, he always rolled again onto his back. He must have tried it a hundred times, closing his eyes, so that he would not have to see the wriggling legs, and gave up only when he began to feel a light, dull pain in his side which he had never felt before.

"O God," he thought, "what a demanding job I've chosen! Day in, day out on the road. The stresses of trade are much greater than the work going on at head office, and, in addition to that, I have to deal with the problems of traveling, the worries about train connections, irregular bad food, temporary and constantly changing human relationships which never come from the heart. To hell with it all!" He felt a slight itching on the top of his abdomen. He slowly pushed himself on his back closer to the bed post so that he could lift his head more easily, found the itchy part, which was entirely covered with small white spots (he did not know what to make of them), and wanted to feel the place with a leg. But he retracted it immediately, for the contact felt like a cold shower all over him.

He slid back again into his earlier position. "This getting up early," he thought, "makes a man quite idiotic. A man must have his sleep. Other traveling salesmen live like harem women. For instance, when I come back to the inn during the course of the morning to write up the necessary orders, these gentlemen are just sitting down to breakfast. If I were to try that with my boss, I'd be thrown out on the spot. Still, who knows whether that mightn't be really good for me. If I didn't hold back for my parents' sake, I would've quit ages ago. I would've gone to the boss and told him just what I think from the bottom of my heart. He would've fallen right off his desk! How weird it is to sit up at the desk and talk down to the employee from way up there. The boss has trouble hearing, so the employee has to step up quite close to him. Anyway, I haven't completely given up that hope yet. Once I've got together the money to pay off the parents' debt to him—that should take another five or six years—I'll do it for sure. Then I'll make the big break. In any case, right now I have to get up. My train leaves at five o'clock.

And he looked over at the alarm clock ticking away by the chest of drawers. "Good God," he thought. It was half past six, and the hands were going quietly on. It was past the half hour, already nearly quarter to. Could the alarm have failed to ring? One saw from the bed that it was properly set for four o'clock. Certainly it had rung. Yes, but was it possible to sleep through this noise that made the furniture shake? Now, it's true he'd not slept quietly, but evidently he'd slept all the more deeply. Still, what should he do now? The next train left at seven o'clock.

To catch that one, he would have to go in a mad rush.

The sample collection wasn't packed up yet, and he really didn't feel particularly fresh and active. And even if he caught the train, there was no avoiding a blow up with the boss, because the firm's errand boy would've waited for the five o'clock train and reported the news of his absence long ago. He was the boss's minion, without backbone or intelligence. Well then, what if he reported in sick? But that would be extremely embarrassing and suspicious, because during his five years' service Gregor hadn't been sick even once. The boss would certainly come with the doctor from the health insurance company and would reproach his parents for their lazy son and cut short all objections with the insurance doctor's comments; for him everyone was completely healthy but really lazy about work. And besides, would the doctor in this case be totally wrong? Apart from a really excessive drowsiness after the long sleep, Gregor in fact felt quite well and even had a really strong appetite.

As he was thinking all this over in the greatest haste, without being able to make the decision to get out of bed (the alarm clock was indicating exactly quarter to seven) there was a cautious knock on the door by the head of the bed.

"Gregor," a voice called (it was his mother!) "it's quarter to seven. Don't you want to be on your way?"

The soft voice! Gregor was startled when he heard his voice answering. It was clearly and unmistakably his earlier voice, but in it was intermingled, as if from below, an irrepressibly painful squeaking which left the words positively distinct only in the first moment and distorted them in the reverberation, so that one didn't know if one had heard correctly.

CHAPTER I

Gregor wanted to answer in detail and explain everything, but in these circumstances he confined himself to saying, "Yes, yes, thank you mother. I'm getting up right away."

Because of the wooden door the change in Gregor's voice was not really noticeable outside, so his mother calmed down with this explanation and shuffled off. However, as a result of the short conversation the other family members became aware of the fact that Gregor was unexpectedly still at home, and already his father was knocking on one side door, weakly but with his fist.

"Gregor, Gregor," he called out, "what's going on?" And after a short while he urged him on again in a deeper voice.

"Gregor! Gregor!" At the other side door, however, his sister knocked lightly. "Gregor? Are you all right? Do you need anything?"

Gregor directed answers in both directions, "I'll be ready right away." He made an effort with the most careful articulation and by inserting long pauses between the individual words to remove everything remarkable from his voice. His father turned back to his breakfast. However, the sister whispered, "Gregor, open the door, I beg you." Gregor had no intention of opening the door, but congratulated himself on his precaution, acquired from traveling, of locking all doors during the night, even at home.

First he wanted to stand up quietly and undisturbed, get dressed, above all have breakfast, and only then consider further action, for (he noticed this clearly) by thinking things over in bed he would not reach a reasonable conclusion. He remembered that he had already often felt a light pain or other in bed, perhaps the result of an awkward lying position, which later turned out to be purely imaginary when he stood up, and he was eager to see how his present fantasies would gradually dissipate.

That the change in his voice was nothing other than the onset of a real chill, an occupational illness of commercial travelers, of that he had not the slightest doubt.

It was very easy to throw aside the blanket. He needed only to push himself up a little, and it fell by itself. But to continue was difficult, particularly because he was so unusually wide. He needed arms and hands to push himself upright. Instead of these, however, he had only many small limbs which were incessantly moving with very different motions and which, in addition, he was unable to control. If he wanted to bend one of them, then it was the first to extend itself, and if he finally succeeded doing with this limb what he wanted, in the meantime all the others, as if left free, moved around in an excessively painful agitation.

"But I must not stay in bed uselessly," said Gregor to

himself.

At first he wanted to get of the bed with the lower part of his body, but this lower part (which he incidentally had not yet looked at and which he also couldn't picture clearly) proved itself too difficult to move. The attempt went so slowly. When, having become almost frantic, he finally hurled himself forward with all his force and without thinking, he chose his direction incorrectly, and he hit the lower bedpost hard. The violent pain he felt revealed to him that the lower part of his body was at the moment probably the most sensitive.

Thus, he tried to get his upper body out of the bed first and turned his head carefully toward the edge of the bed.

He managed to do this easily, and in spite of its width and weight his body mass at last slowly followed the turning of his head. But as he finally raised his head outside the bed in the open air, he became anxious about moving forward any further in this manner, for if he allowed himself eventually to fall by this process, it would take a miracle to prevent his head from getting injured. And at all costs he must not lose consciousness right now. He preferred to remain in bed.

However, after a similar effort, while he lay there again sighing as before and once again saw his small limbs fighting one another, if anything worse than before, and didn't see any chance of imposing quiet and order on this arbitrary movement, he told himself again that he couldn't possibly remain in bed and that it might be the most reasonable thing to sacrifice everything if there was even the slightest hope of getting himself out of bed in the process. At the same moment, however, he didn't forget to remind himself from time to time of the fact that calm (indeed the calmest) reflection might be better than the most confused decisions. At such moments, he directed his gaze as precisely as he could toward the window, but unfortunately there was little confident cheer to be had from a glance at the morning mist, which concealed even the other side of the narrow street. "It's already seven o'clock" he told himself at the latest striking of the alarm clock, "already seven o'clock and still such a fog." And for a little while longer he lay quietly with weak breathing, as if perhaps waiting for normal and natural conditions to re-emerge out of the complete stillness.

But then he said to himself, "Before it strikes a quarter past seven, whatever happens I must be completely out of bed. Besides, by then someone from the office will arrive to inquire about me, because the office will open before seven o'clock." And he made an effort then to rock his entire body length out of the bed with a uniform motion.

If he let himself fall out of the bed in this way, his

head, which in the course of the fall he intended to lift up sharply, would probably remain uninjured. His back seemed to be hard; nothing would really happen to that as a result of the fall. His greatest reservation was a worry about the loud noise which the fall must create and which presumably would arouse, if not fright, then at least concern on the other side of all the doors. However, it had to be tried.

As Gregor was in the process of lifting himself half out of bed (the new method was more of a game than an effort; he needed only to rock with a constant rhythm) it struck him how easy all this would be if someone were to come to his aid. Two strong people (he thought of his father and the servant girl) would have been quite sufficient. They would have only had to push their arms under his arched back to get him out of the bed, to bend down with their load, and then merely to exercise patience and care that he completed the flip onto the floor, where his diminutive legs would then, he hoped, acquire a purpose. Now, quite apart from the fact that the doors were locked, should he really call out for help? In spite of all his distress, he was unable to suppress a smile at this idea.

He had already got to the point where, with a stronger rocking, he maintained his equilibrium with difficulty, and very soon he would finally have to decide, for in five minutes it would be a quarter past seven. Then there was a ring at the door of the apartment. "That's someone from the office" he told himself, and he almost froze while his small limbs only danced around all the faster. For one moment everything remained still.

"They aren't opening," Gregor said to himself, caught up in some absurd hope.

But of course then, as usual, the servant girl with her firm tread went to the door and opened it. Gregor needed to hear only the visitor's first word of greeting to recognize immediately who it was, the manager himself. Why was Gregor the only one condemned to work in a firm where at the slightest lapse someone immediately attracted the greatest suspicion? Were all the employees then collectively, one and all, scoundrels? Was there then among them no truly devoted person who, if he failed to use just a couple of hours in the morning for office work, would become abnormal from pangs of conscience and really be in no state to get out of bed? Was it really not enough to let an apprentice make inquiries, if such questioning was even necessary? Must the manager himself come, and in the process must it be demonstrated to the entire innocent family that the investigation of this suspicious circumstance could only be entrusted to the intelligence of the manager?

And more as a consequence of the excited state in which this idea put Gregor than as a result of an actual decision, he swung himself with all his might out of the bed. There was a loud thud, but not a real crash. The fall was absorbed somewhat by the carpet and, in addition, his back was more elastic than Gregor had thought. For that reason the dull noise was not quite so conspicuous. But he had not held his head up with sufficient care and had hit it. He turned his head, irritated and in pain, and rubbed it on the carpet.

"Something has fallen in there," said the manager in the next room on the left.

Gregor tried to imagine to himself whether anything similar to what was happening to him today could have also happened at some point to the manager. At least one had to concede the possibility of such a thing. However, as if to give a rough answer to this question, the manager now took a few determined steps in the next room, with a squeak of his polished boots.

From the neighbouring room on the right the sister was whispering to inform Gregor: "Gregor, the manager is here."

"I know," said Gregor to himself. But he did not dare make his voice loud enough so that his sister could hear.

"Gregor," his father now said from the neighbouring room on the left, "Mr. Manager has come and is asking why you have not left on the early train. We don't know what we should tell him. Besides, he also wants to speak to you personally. So please open the door. He will good enough to forgive the mess in your room."

In the middle of all this, the manager called out in a friendly way, "Good morning, Mr. Samsa."

"He is not well," said his mother to the manager, while his father was still talking at the door, "He is not well, believe me, Mr. Manager. Otherwise how would Gregor miss a train! The young man has nothing in his head except business. I'm almost angry that he never goes out at night. Right now he's been in the city eight days, but he's been at home every evening. He sits there with us at the table and reads the newspaper quietly or studies his travel schedules. It's quite a diversion for him if he busies himself with fretwork. For instance, he cut out a small frame over the course of two or three evenings. You'd be amazed how pretty it is. It's hanging right inside the room. You'll see it immediately, as soon as Gregor opens the door. Anyway, I'm happy that you're here, Mr. Manager. By ourselves, we would never have made Gregor open the door. He's so stubborn, and he's certainly not well, although he denied that this morning."

"I'm coming right away," said Gregor slowly and deliberately and didn't move, so as not to lose one word of the conversation.

"My dear lady, I cannot explain it to myself in any other way," said the manager; "I hope it is nothing serious. On the other hand, I must also say that we business people, luckily or unluckily, however one looks at it, very often simply have to overcome a slight indisposition for business reasons."

"So can Mr. Manager come in to see you now" asked his father impatiently and knocked once again on the door.

"No," said Gregor. In the neighbouring room on the left a painful stillness descended. In the neighbouring room on the right the sister began to sob.

Why didn't his sister go to the others? She'd probably just gotten up out of bed now and hadn't even started to get dressed yet. Then why was she crying? Because he wasn't getting up and wasn't letting the manager in; because he was in danger of losing his position, and because then his boss would badger his parents once again with the old demands? Those were probably unnecessary worries right now. Gregor was still here and wasn't thinking at all about abandoning his family. At the moment he was lying right there on the carpet, and no one who knew about his condition would've seriously demanded that he let the manager in. But Gregor wouldn't be casually dismissed right way because of this small discourtesy, for which he would find an easy and suitable excuse later on. It seemed to Gregor that it might be far more reasonable to leave him in peace at the moment, instead of disturbing him with crying and conversation. But it was the very uncertainty which distressed the others and excused their behaviour.

"Mr. Samsa," the manager was now shouting, his voice raised, "what's the matter? You are barricading yourself in your room, answer with only a yes and a no, are making serious and unnecessary troubles for your parents, and neglecting (I mention this only incidentally) your commercial duties in a truly unheard of manner. I am speaking here in the name of your parents and your employer, and I am requesting you in all seriousness for an immediate and clear explanation. I am amazed. I am amazed. I thought I knew you as a calm, reasonable person, and now you appear suddenly to want to start parading around in weird moods. The Chief indicated to me earlier this very day a possible explanation for your neglect—it concerned the collection of cash entrusted to you a short while ago—but in truth I almost gave him my word of honour that this explanation could not be correct. However, now I see here your unimaginable pig headedness, and I am totally losing any desire to speak up for you in the slightest. And your position is not at all the most secure. Originally I intended to mention all this to you privately, but since you are letting me waste my time here uselessly, I don't know why the matter shouldn't come to the attention of your parents. Your productivity has also been very unsatisfactory recently. Of course, it's not the time of year to conduct exceptional business, we recognize that, but a time of year for conducting no business, there is no such thing at all, Mr. Samsa, and such a thing must never be."

"But Mr. Manager," called Gregor, beside himself and in his agitation forgetting everything else, "I'm opening the door immediately, this very moment. A slight indisposition, a dizzy spell, has prevented me from getting up. I'm still lying in bed right now. But now I'm quite refreshed once again. I'm in the midst of getting out of bed. Just have patience for a short moment! Things are not going so well as I thought. But things are all right. How suddenly this can overcome someone! Just yesterday evening everything was fine with me. My parents certainly know that. Actually just yesterday evening I had a small premonition. People must have seen that in me. Why have I not reported that to the office! But people always think that they'll get over sickness without having to stay at home. Mr. Manager! Take it easy on my parents! There is really no basis for the criticisms which you are now making against me, and really nobody has said a word to me about that. Perhaps you have not read the latest orders which I shipped. Besides, now I'm setting out on my trip on the eight o'clock train; the few hours' rest have made me stronger. Mr. Manager, do not stay. I will be at the office in person right away. Please have the goodness to say that and to convey my respects to the Chief."

While Gregor was quickly blurting all this out, hardly aware of what he was saying, he had moved close to the chest of drawers without effort, probably as a result of the practice he had already had in bed, and now he was trying to raise himself up on it. Actually, he wanted to open the door; he really wanted to let himself be seen by and to speak with the manager. He was keen to witness what the others now asking after him would say at the sight of him.

If they were startled, then Gregor had no more responsibility and could be calm. But if they accepted everything quietly, then he would have no reason to get excited and, if he got a move on, could really be at the station around eight o'clock.

At first he slid down a few times from the smooth chest of drawers. But at last he gave himself a final swing and stood upright there. He was no longer at all aware of the pains in his lower body, no matter how they might still sting. Now he let himself fall against the back of a nearby chair, on the edge of which he braced himself with his thin limbs. By doing this he gained control over himself and kept quiet, for he could now hear the manager.

"Did you understood a single word?" the manager asked the parents, "Is he playing the fool with us?"

"For God's sake," cried the mother already in tears, "perhaps he's very ill and we're upsetting him. Grete! Grete!" she yelled at that point.

"Mother?" called the sister from the other side. They were making themselves understood through Gregor's room.

"You must go to the doctor right away. Gregor is sick. Hurry to the doctor. Have you heard Gregor speak yet?"

"That was an animal's voice," said the manager, remarkably quietly in comparison to the mother's cries.

"Anna! Anna!" yelled the father through the hall into the kitchen, clapping his hands, "fetch a locksmith right away!"

The two young women were already running through the hall with swishing skirts (how had his sister dressed herself so quickly?) and yanked open the doors of the apartment. One couldn't hear the doors closing at all. They probably had left them open, as is customary in an apartment in which a huge misfortune has taken place.

However, Gregor had become much calmer. All right, people did not understand his words any more, although they seemed clear enough to him, clearer than previously, perhaps because his ears had gotten used to them. But at least people now thought that things were not all right with him and were prepared to help him. The confidence and assurance with which the first arrangements had been carried out made him feel good. He felt himself included once again in the circle of humanity and was expecting from both the doctor and the locksmith, without differentiating between them with any real precision, splendid and surprising results. In order to get as clear a voice as possible for the critical conversation which was imminent, he coughed a little, and certainly took the trouble to do this in a really subdued way, since it was possible that even this noise sounded like something different from a human cough. He no longer trusted himself to decide any more. Meanwhile in the next room it had become really quiet. Perhaps his parents were sitting with the manager at the table and were whispering; perhaps they were all leaning against the door and listening.

Gregor pushed himself slowly towards the door, with the help of the easy chair, let go of it there, threw himself against the door, held himself upright against it (the balls of his tiny limbs had a little sticky stuff on them), and rested there momentarily from his exertion. Then he made an effort to turn the key in the lock with his mouth. Unfortunately it seemed that he had no real teeth. How then was he to grab hold of the key? But to make up for that his jaws were naturally very strong; with their help he managed to get the key really moving, and he did not notice that he was obviously inflicting some damage on himself, for a brown fluid came out of his mouth, flowed over the key, and dripped onto the floor.

"Just listen for a moment," said the manager in the

next room, "he's turning the key."

For Gregor that was a great encouragement. But they all should've called out to him, including his father and mother, "Come on, Gregor," they should've shouted, "keep going, keep working on the lock." Imagining that all his efforts were being followed with suspense, he bit down frantically on the key with all the force he could muster. As the key turned more, he danced around the lock. Now he was holding himself upright only with his mouth, and he had to hang onto the key or then press it down again with the whole weight of his body, as necessary. The quite distinct click of the lock as it finally snapped really woke Gregor up. Breathing heavily he said to himself, "So I didn't need the locksmith," and he set his head against the door handle to open the door completely.

Because he had to open the door in this way, it was already open very wide without him yet being really visible. He first had to turn himself slowly around the edge of the door, very carefully, of course, if he did not want to fall awkwardly on his back right at the entrance into the room. He was still preoccupied with this difficult movement and had no time to pay attention to anything else, when he heard the manager exclaim a loud "Oh!" (it sounded like the wind whistling), and now he saw him, nearest to the door, pressing his hand against his open mouth and moving slowly back, as if an invisible constant force was pushing him away. His mother (in spite of the presence of the manager she was standing here with her hair sticking up on end, still a mess from the night) with her hands clasped was looking at his father; she then went two steps towards Gregor and collapsed right in the middle of her skirts spreading out all around her, her face sunk on her breast, completely concealed. His father clenched his fist with a hostile expression, as if he wished to push Gregor back into his room, then looked uncertainly around the living room, covered his eyes with his hands, and cried so that his mighty breast shook.

At this point Gregor did not take one step into the room, but leaned his body from the inside against the firmly bolted wing of the door, so that only half his body was visible, as well as his head, titled sideways, with which he peeped over at the others. Meanwhile it had become much brighter. Standing out clearly from the other side of the street was a part of the endless gray-black house situated opposite (it was a hospital) with its severe regular windows breaking up the facade. The rain was still coming down, but only in large individual drops visibly and firmly thrown down one by one onto the ground. The breakfast dishes were standing piled around on the table, because for his father breakfast was the most important meal time in the day, which he prolonged for hours by reading various newspapers. Directly across on the opposite wall hung a photograph of Gregor from the time of his military service; it was a picture of him as a lieutenant, as he, smiling and worry free, with his hand on his sword, demanded respect for his bearing and uniform. The door to the hall was ajar, and since the door to the apartment was also open, one saw out into the landing of the apartment and the start of the staircase going down.

"Now," said Gregor, well aware that he was the only one who had kept his composure. "I'll get dressed right away, pack up the collection of samples, and set off. You'll allow me to set out on my way, will you not? You see, Mr. Manager, I am not pig-headed, and I am happy to work. Traveling is exhausting, but I couldn't live without it.

Where are you going, Mr. Manager? To the office? Really? Will you report everything truthfully? A person can be incapable of work momentarily, but that is precisely the best time to remember the earlier achievements and to consider that later, after the obstacles have been shoved aside, the person will work all the more keenly and intensely. I am really so indebted to Mr. Chief—you know that perfectly well. On the other hand, I am concerned about my parents and my sister. I'm in a fix, but I'll work myself out of it again. Don't make things more difficult for me than they already are. Speak up on my behalf in the office! People don't like traveling salesmen. I know that. People think they earn pots of money and thus lead a fine life. People don't even have any special reason to think through this judgment more clearly. But you, Mr. Manager, you have a better perspective on the interconnections than the other people, even, I tell you in total confidence, a better perspective than Mr. Chairman himself, who in his capacity as the employer may let his judgment make casual mistakes at the expense of an employee. You also know well enough that the traveling salesman who is outside the office almost the entire year can become so easily a victim of gossip, coincidences, and groundless complaints, against which it's impossible for him to defend himself, since for the most part he doesn't hear about them at all and only then when he's exhausted after finishing a trip, and gets to feel in his own body at home the nasty consequences, which can't be thoroughly explored back to their origins. Mr. Manager, don't leave without speaking a word telling me that you'll at least concede that I'm a little in the right!"

But at Gregor's first words the manager had already turned away, and now he looked back at Gregor over his twitching shoulders with pursed lips. During Gregor's speech he was not still for a moment, but was moving away towards the door, without taking his eyes off Gregor, but really gradually, as if there was a secret ban on leaving the room. He was already in the hall, and after the sudden movement with which he finally pulled his foot out of the living room, one could have believed that he had just burned the sole of his foot. In the hall, however, he stretched out his right hand away from his body towards the staircase, as if some truly supernatural relief was waiting for him there.

Gregor realized that he must not under any circumstances allow the manager to go away in this frame of mind, especially if his position in the firm was not to be placed in the greatest danger. His parents did not understand all this very well. Over the long years, they had developed the conviction that Gregor was set up for life in his firm and, in addition, they had so much to do nowadays with their present troubles that all foresight was foreign to them. But Gregor had this foresight. The manager must be held back, calmed down, convinced, and finally won over. The future of Gregor and his family really depended on it! If only the sister had been there! She was clever. She had already cried while Gregor was still lying quietly on his back. And the manager, this friend of the ladies, would certainly let himself be guided by her. She would have closed the door to the apartment and talked him out of his fright in the hall. But the sister was not even there. Gregor must deal with it himself.

Without thinking that as yet he didn't know anything about his present ability to move and without thinking that his speech possibly (indeed probably) had once again not been understood, he left the wing of the door, pushed himself through the opening, and wanted to go over to the manager, who was already holding tight onto the handrail with both hands on the landing in a ridiculous way. But as he looked for something to hold onto, with a small scream Gregor immediately fell down onto his numerous little legs. Scarcely had this happened, when he felt for the first time that morning a general physical well being. The small limbs had firm floor under them; they obeyed perfectly, as he noticed to his joy, and strove to carry him forward in the direction he wanted. Right away he believed that the final amelioration of all his suffering was immediately at hand. But at the very moment when he lay on the floor rocking in a restrained manner quite close and directly across from his mother (apparently totally sunk into herself) she suddenly sprang right up with her arms spread far apart and her fingers extended and cried out, "Help, for God's sake, help!" She held her head bowed down, as if she wanted to view Gregor better, but ran senselessly back, contradicting that gesture, forgetting that behind her stood the table with all the dishes on it. When she reached the table, she sat down heavily on it, as if absent-mindedly, and did not appear to notice at all that next to her coffee was pouring out onto the carpet in a full stream from the large overturned container.

"Mother, mother," said Gregor quietly, and looked over towards her. The manager momentarily had disappeared completely from his mind; by contrast, at the sight of the flowing coffee he couldn't stop himself snapping his jaws in the air a few times. At that his mother screamed all over again, hurried from the table, and collapsed into the arms of his father, who was rushing towards her. But Gregor had no time right now for his parents: the manager was already on the staircase. His chin level with the banister, the manager looked back for the last time. Gregor took an initial movement to catch up to him if possible. But the manager must have suspected something, because he made a leap down over a few stairs and disappeared, still shouting "Huh!" The sound echoed throughout the entire stairwell.

Now, unfortunately this flight of the manager also seemed completely to bewilder his father, who earlier had been relatively calm, for instead of running after the manager himself or at least not hindering Gregor from his pursuit, with his right hand he grabbed hold of the manager's cane, which he had left behind with his hat and overcoat on a chair. With his left hand, his father picked up a large newspaper from the table and, stamping his feet on the floor, he set out to drive Gregor back into his room by waving the cane and the newspaper. No request of Gregor's was of any use; no request would even be understood. No matter how willing he was to turn his head respectfully, his father just stomped all the harder with his feet.

Across the room from him his mother had pulled open a window, in spite of the cool weather, and leaning out with her hands on her cheeks, she pushed her face far outside the window. Between the alley and the stair well a strong draught came up, the curtains on the window flew around, the newspapers on the table swished, and individual sheets fluttered down over the floor. The father relentlessly pressed forward pushing out sibilants, like a wild man. Now, Gregor had no practice at all in going backwards; it was really going very slowly. If Gregor only had been allowed to turn himself around, he would have been in his room right away, but he was afraid to make his father impatient by the time-consuming process of turning around, and each moment he faced the threat of a mortal blow on his back or his head from the cane in his father's hand. Finally Gregor had no other option, for he noticed with horror that he did not understand yet how to maintain his direction going backwards. And so he began, amid constantly anxious sideways glances in his father's direction, to turn himself around as quickly as possible (although in truth this was only very slowly). Perhaps his father noticed his good intentions, for he did not disrupt Gregor in this motion, but with the tip of the cane from a distance he even directed here and there Gregor's rotating movement.

If only there hadn't been his father's unbearable hissing!

Because of that Gregor totally lost his head. He was already almost totally turned around, when, always with this hissing in his ear, he just made a mistake and turned himself back a little. But when he finally was successful in getting his head in front of the door opening, it became clear that his body was too wide to go through any further. Naturally his father, in his present mental state, had no idea of opening the other wing of the door a bit to create a suitable passage for Gregor to get through. His single fixed thought was that Gregor must get into his room as quickly as possible. He would never have allowed the elaborate preparations that Gregor required to orient himself and thus perhaps get through the door. On the contrary, as if there were no obstacle and with a peculiar noise, he now drove Gregor forwards. Behind Gregor the sound was at this point no longer like the voice of only a single father. Now it was really no longer a joke, and Gregor forced himself, come what might, into the door. One side of his body was lifted up. He lay at an angle in the door opening. His one flank was sore with the scraping. On the white door ugly blotches were left. Soon he was stuck fast and would have not been able to move any more on his own. The tiny legs on one side hung twitching in the air above, the ones on the other side were pushed painfully into the floor. Then his father gave him one really strong liberating push from behind, and he scurried, bleeding severely, far into the interior of his room. The door was slammed shut with the cane, and finally it was quiet.

CHAPTER II

Gregor first woke up from his heavy swoon-like sleep in the evening twilight. He would certainly have woken up soon afterwards without any disturbance, for he felt himself sufficiently rested and wide awake, although it appeared to him as if a hurried step and a cautious closing of the door to the hall had aroused him. The shine of the electric streetlights lay pale here and there on the ceiling and on the higher parts of the furniture, but underneath around Gregor it was dark. He pushed himself slowly toward the door, still groping awkwardly with his feelers, which he now learned to value for the first time, to check what was happening there. His left side seemed one single long unpleasantly stretched scar, and he really had to hobble on his two rows of legs. In addition, one small leg had been seriously wounded in the course of the morning incident (it was almost a miracle that only one had been hurt) and dragged lifelessly behind.

By the door he first noticed what had really lured him there: it was the smell of something to eat. For there stood a bowl filled with sweetened milk, in which swam tiny pieces of white bread. He almost laughed with joy, for he now had a much greater hunger than in the morning, and he immediately dipped his head almost up to and over his eyes down into the milk. But he soon drew it back again in disappointment, not just because it was difficult for him to eat on account of his delicate left side (he could eat only if his entire panting body worked in a coordinated way), but also because the milk, which otherwise was his favorite drink and which his sister had certainly placed there for that reason, did not appeal to him at all. He turned away from the bowl almost with aversion and crept back into the middle of the room.

In the living room, as Gregor saw through the crack in the door, the gas was lit, but where on other occasions at this time of day the father was accustomed to read the afternoon newspaper in a loud voice to his mother and sometimes also to his sister, at the moment not a sound was audible. Now, perhaps this reading aloud, about which his sister always spoken and written to him, had recently fallen out of their general routine. But it was so still all around, in spite of the fact that the apartment was certainly not empty. "What a quiet life the family leads", said Gregor to himself and, as he stared fixedly out in front of him into the darkness, he felt a great pride that he had been able to provide such a life in a beautiful apartment like this for his parents and his sister. But how would things go if now all tranquillity, all prosperity, all contentment should come to a horrible end? In order not to lose himself in such thoughts, Gregor preferred to set himself moving and crawled up and down in his room.

Once during the long evening one side door and then the other door was opened just a tiny crack and quickly closed again. Someone presumably needed to come in but had then thought better of it. Gregor immediately took up a position by the living room door, determined to bring in the hesitant visitor somehow or other or at least to find out who it might be. But now the door was not opened any more, and Gregor waited in vain. Earlier, when the door had been barred, they had all wanted to come in to him; now, when he had opened one door and when the others had obviously been opened during the day, no one came any more, and the keys were stuck in the locks on the outside.

The light in the living room was turned off only late at night, and now it was easy to establish that his parents and his sister had stayed awake all this time, for one could hear clearly as all three moved away on tiptoe. Now it was certain that no one would come into Gregor any more until the morning. Thus, he had a long time to think undisturbed about how he should reorganize his life from scratch. But the high, open room, in which he was compelled to lie flat on the floor, made him anxious, without his being able to figure out the reason, for he had lived in the room for five years. With a half unconscious turn and not without a slight shame he scurried under the couch, where, in spite of the fact that his back was a little cramped and he could no longer lift up his head, he felt very comfortable and was sorry only that his body was too wide to fit completely under it.

There he remained the entire night, which he spent partly in a state of semi-sleep, out of which his hunger constantly woke him with a start, but partly in a state of worry and murky hopes, which all led to the conclusion that for the time being he would have to keep calm and with patience and the greatest consideration for his family tolerate the troubles which in his present condition he was now forced to cause them.

Already early in the morning (it was still almost night) Gregor had an opportunity to test the power of the decisions he had just made, for his sister, almost fully dressed, opened the door from the hall into his room and looked eagerly inside. She did not find him immediately, but when she noticed him under the couch (God, he had to be somewhere or other; for he could hardly fly away) she got such a shock that, without being able to control herself, she slammed the door shut once again from the outside. However, as if she was sorry for her behaviour, she immediately opened the door again and walked in on her tiptoes, as if she was in the presence of a serious invalid or a total stranger. Gregor had pushed his head forward just to the edge of the couch and was observing her. Would she really notice that he had left the milk standing, not indeed from any lack of hunger, and would she bring in something else to eat more suitable for him? If she did not do it on her own, he would sooner starve to death than call her attention to the fact, although he had a really powerful urge to move beyond the couch, throw himself at his sister's feet, and beg her for something or other good to eat. But his sister noticed right away with astonishment that the bowl was still full, with only a little milk spilled around it. She picked it up immediately (although not with her bare hands but with a rag), and took it out of the room. Gregor was extremely curious what she would bring as a substitute, and he pictured to himself different ideas about that. But he never could have guessed what his sister out of the goodness of her heart in fact did. She brought him, to test his taste, an entire selection, all spread out on an old newspaper. There were old half-rotten vegetables, bones from the evening meal, covered with a white sauce which had almost solidified, some raisins and almonds, cheese, which Gregor had declared inedible two days earlier, a slice of dry bread, a slice of salted bread smeared with butter. In addition to all this, she put down a bowl (probably designated once and for all as Gregor's) into which she had poured some water. And out of her delicacy of feeling, since she knew that Gregor would not eat in front of her, she went away very quickly and even turned the key in the lock, so that Gregor could now observe that he could make himself as comfortable as he wished. Gregor's small limbs buzzed as the time for eating had come. His wounds must, in any case, have already healed completely. He felt no handicap on that score. He was astonished at that and thought about it, how more than a month ago he had cut his finger slightly with a knife and how this wound had hurt enough even the day before yesterday.

"Am I now going to be less sensitive," he thought, already sucking greedily on the cheese, which had strongly attracted him right away, more than all the other foods. Quickly and with his eyes watering with satisfaction, he ate one after the other the cheese, the vegetables, and the sauce; the fresh food, by contrast, didn't taste good to him. He couldn't bear the smell and even carried the things he wanted to eat a little distance away. By the time his sister slowly turned the key as a sign that he should withdraw, he was long finished and now lay lazily in the same spot. The noise immediately startled him, in spite of the fact that he was already almost asleep, and he scurried back again under the couch. But it cost him great self-control to remain under the couch, even for the short time his sister was in the room, because his body had filled out somewhat on account of the rich meal and in the narrow space there he could scarcely breathe. In the midst of minor attacks of asphyxiation, he looked at her with somewhat protruding eyes, as his unsuspecting sister swept up with a broom, not just the remnants, but even the foods which Gregor had not touched at all, as if these were also now useless, and as she dumped everything quickly into a bucket, which she closed with a wooden lid, and then carried all of it out of the room. She had hardly turned around before Gregor had already dragged himself out from the couch, stretched out, and let his body expand.

In this way Gregor got his food every day, once in the morning, when his parents and the servant girl were still asleep, and a second time after the common noon meal, for his parents were, as before, asleep then for a little while, and the servant girl was sent off by his sister on some errand or other. Certainly they would not have wanted Gregor to starve to death, but perhaps they could not have endured finding out what he ate other than by hearsay. Perhaps his sister wanted to spare them what was possibly only a small grief, for they were really suffering quite enough already.

What sorts of excuses people had used on that first morning to get the doctor and the locksmith out of the house Gregor was completely unable to ascertain. Since he was not comprehensible, no one, not even his sister, thought that he might be able to understand others, and thus, when his sister was in her room, he had to be content with listening now and then to her sighs and invocations to the saints. Only later, when she had grown somewhat accustomed to everything (naturally there could never be any talk of her growing completely accustomed to it) Gregor sometimes caught a comment which was intended to be friendly or could be interpreted as such.

"Well, today it tasted good to him," she said, if Gregor had really cleaned up what he had to eat; whereas, in the reverse situation, which gradually repeated itself more and more frequently, she used to say sadly, "Now everything has stopped again."

But while Gregor could get no new information directly, he did hear a good deal from the room next door, and as soon as he heard voices, he scurried right away to the relevant door and pressed his entire body against it. In the early days especially, there was no conversation which was not concerned with him in some way or other, even if only in secret. For two days at all meal times discussions on that subject could be heard on how people should now behave; but they also talked about the same subject in the times between meals, for there were always at least two family members at home, since no one really wanted to remain in the house alone and people could not under any circumstances leave the apartment completely empty. In addition, on the very first day the servant girl (it was not completely clear what and how much she knew about what had happened) on her knees had begged his mother to let her go immediately, and when she said good bye about fifteen minutes later, she thanked them for the dismissal with tears in her eyes, as if she was receiving the greatest favour which people had shown her there, and, without anyone demanding it from her, she swore a fearful oath not to betray anyone, not even the slightest bit.

Now his sister had to team up with his mother to do the cooking, although that didn't create much trouble because people were eating almost nothing. Again and again Gregor listened as one of them vainly invited another one to eat and received no answer other than "Thank you. I have enough" or something like that. And perhaps they had stopped having anything to drink, too. His sister often asked his father whether he wanted to have a beer and gladly offered to fetch it herself, and when his father was silent, she said, in order to remove any reservations he might have, that she could send the caretaker's wife to get it. But then his father finally said a resounding "No," and nothing more would be spoken about it.

Already during the first day his father laid out all the financial circumstances and prospects to his mother and to his sister as well. From time to time he stood up from the table and pulled out of the small lockbox salvaged from his business, which had collapsed five years previously, some document or other or some notebook. The sound was audible as he opened up the complicated lock and, after removing what he was looking for, locked it up again. These explanations by his father were, in part, the first enjoyable thing that Gregor had the chance to listen to since his imprisonment. He had thought that nothing at all was left over for his father from that business; at least his father had told him nothing to the contradict that view, and Gregor in any case hadn't asked him about it. At the time Gregor's only concern had been to devote everything he had in order to allow his family to forget as quickly as possible the business misfortune which had brought them all into a state of complete hopelessness. And so at that point he'd started to work with a special intensity and from an assistant had become, almost overnight, a traveling salesman, who naturally had entirely different possibilities for earning money and whose successes at work at once were converted into the form of cash commissions, which could be set out on the table at home in front of his astonished and delighted family.

Those had been beautiful days, and they had never come back afterwards, at least not with the same splendour, in spite of the fact that Gregor later earned so much money that he was in a position to bear the expenses of the

entire family, expenses which he, in fact, did bear. They had become quite accustomed to it, both the family and Gregor as well. They took the money with thanks, and he happily surrendered it, but the special warmth was no longer present. Only the sister had remained still close to Gregor, and it was his secret plan to send her (in contrast to Gregor she loved music very much and knew how to play the violin charmingly) next year to the conservatory, regardless of the great expense which that must necessitate and which would be made up in other ways. Now and then during Gregor's short stays in the city the conservatory was mentioned in conversations with his sister, but always only as a beautiful dream, whose realization was unimaginable, and their parents never listened to these innocent expectations with pleasure. But Gregor thought about them with scrupulous consideration and intended to explain the matter ceremoniously on Christmas Eve.

In his present situation, such futile ideas went through his head, while he pushed himself right up against the door and listened. Sometimes in his general exhaustion he couldn't listen any more and let his head bang listlessly against the door, but he immediately pulled himself together, for even the small sound which he made by this motion was heard near by and silenced everyone. " There he goes on again," said his father after a while, clearly turning towards the door, and only then would the interrupted conversation gradually be resumed again.

Gregor found out clearly enough (for his father tended to repeat himself often in his explanations, partly because he had not personally concerned himself with these matters for a long time now, and partly also because his mother did not understand everything right away the first time) that, in spite all bad luck, a fortune, although a very small one, was available from the old times, which the interest (which had not been touched) had in the intervening time gradually allowed to increase a little. Furthermore, in addition to this, the money which Gregor had brought home every month (he had kept only a few florins for himself) had not been completely spent and had grown into a small capital amount. Gregor, behind his door, nodded eagerly, rejoicing over this unanticipated foresight and frugality. True, with this excess money, he could have paid off more of his father's debt to his employer and the day on which he could be rid of this position would have been a lot closer, but now things were doubtless better the way his father had arranged them.

At the moment, however, this money was nowhere near sufficient to permit the family to live on the interest payments. Perhaps it would be enough to maintain the family for one or at most two years, that's all. Thus it came only to an amount which one should not really take out and which must be set aside for an emergency. But the money to live on must be earned. Now, his father was a healthy man, although he was old, who had not worked at all for five years now and thus could not be counted on for very much. He had in these five years, the first holidays of his trouble-filled but unsuccessful life, put on a good deal of fat and thus had become really heavy. And should his old mother now maybe work for money, a woman who suffered from asthma, for whom wandering through the apartment even now was a great strain and who spent every second day on the sofa by the open window labouring for breath? Should his sister earn money, a girl who was still a seventeen-year-old child, whose earlier life style had been so very delightful that it had consisted of dressing herself nicely, sleeping in late, helping around the house, taking part in a few modest enjoyments and, above all, playing the violin? When it came to talking about this need to earn money, at first Gregor went away from the door and threw himself on the cool leather sofa beside the door, for he was quite hot from shame and sorrow.

Often he lay there all night long. He didn't sleep a moment and just scratched on the leather for hours at a time. He undertook the very difficult task of shoving a chair over to the window. Then he crept up on the window sill and, braced in the chair, leaned against the window to look out, obviously with some memory or other of the satisfaction which that used to bring him in earlier times.

Actually from day to day he perceived things with less and less clarity, even those a short distance away: the hospital across the street, the all too frequent sight of which he had previously cursed, was not visible at all any more, and if he had not been precisely aware that he lived in the quiet but completely urban Charlotte Street, he could have believed that from his window he was peering out at a featureless wasteland, in which the gray heaven and the gray earth had merged and were indistinguishable. His attentive sister must have observed a couple of times that the chair stood by the window; then, after cleaning up the room, each time she pushed the chair back right against the window and from now on she even left the inner casement open.

If Gregor had only been able to speak to his sister and thank her for everything that she had to do for him, he would have tolerated her service more easily. As it was he suffered under it. The sister admittedly sought to cover up the awkwardness of everything as much as possible, and, as time went by, she naturally got more successful at it. But with the passing of time Gregor also came to understand everything more precisely. Even her entrance was terrible for him. As soon as she entered, she ran straight to the window, without taking the time to shut the door (in spite of the fact that she was otherwise very considerate in sparing anyone the sight of Gregor's room), and yanked the window open with eager hands, as if she was almost suffocating, and remained for a while by the window breathing deeply, even when it was still so cold. With this running and noise she frightened Gregor twice every day. The entire time he trembled under the couch, and yet he knew very well that she would certainly have spared him gladly if it had only been possible to remain with the window closed in a room where Gregor lived.

On one occasion (about one month had already gone by since Gregor's transformation, and there was now no particular reason any more for his sister to be startled at Gregor's appearance) she came a little earlier than usual and came upon Gregor as he was still looking out the window, immobile and well positioned to frighten someone. It would not have come as a surprise to Gregor if she had not come in, since his position was preventing her from opening the window immediately. But she not only did not step inside; she even retreated and shut the door. A stranger really could have concluded from this that Gregor had been lying in wait for her and wanted to bite her. Of course, Gregor immediately concealed himself under the couch, but he had to wait until the noon meal before his sister returned, and she seemed much less calm than usual. From this he realized that his appearance was still constantly intolerable to her and must remain intolerable in future, and that she really had to exert a lot of self-control not to run away from a glimpse of only the small part of his body which stuck out from under the couch. In order to spare her even this sight, one day he dragged the sheet on his back onto the couch (this task took him four hours) and arranged it in such a way that he was now completely concealed and his sister, even if she bent down, could not see him. If this sheet was not necessary as far as she was concerned, then she could remove it, for it was clear enough that Gregor could not derive any pleasure from isolating himself away so completely. But she left the sheet just as it was, and Gregor believed he even caught a look of gratitude when on one occasion he carefully lifted up the sheet a little with his head to check as his sister took stock of the new arrangement.

In the first two weeks his parents could not bring themselves to visit him, and he often heard how they fully acknowledged his sister's present work; whereas, earlier they had often got annoyed at his sister because she had seemed to them a somewhat useless young woman. However, now both his father and his mother often waited in front of Gregor's door while his sister cleaned up inside, and as soon as she came out she had to explain in detail how things looked in the room, what Gregor had eaten, how he had behaved this time, and whether perhaps a slight improvement was perceptible. In any event, his mother comparatively soon wanted to visit Gregor, but his father and his sister restrained her, at first with reasons which

Gregor listened to very attentively and which he completely endorsed. Later, however, they had to hold her back forcefully, and when she then cried "Let me go to Gregor. He's my unlucky son! Don't you understand that I have to go to him?" Gregor then thought that perhaps it would be a good thing if his mother came in, not every day, of course, but maybe once a week. She understood everything much better than his sister, who in spite of all her courage was still a child and, in the last analysis, had perhaps undertaken such a difficult task only out of childish recklessness.

Gregor's wish to see his mother was soon realized. While during the day Gregor, out of consideration for his parents, did not want to show himself by the window, he couldn't crawl around very much on the few square metres of the floor. He found it difficult to bear lying quietly during the night, and soon eating no longer gave him the slightest pleasure. So for diversion he acquired the habit of crawling back and forth across the walls and ceiling. He was especially fond of hanging from the ceiling. The experience was quite different from lying on the floor. It was easier to breathe, a slight vibration went through his body, and in the midst of the almost happy amusement which Gregor found up there, it could happen that, to his own surprise, he let go and hit the floor.

However, now he naturally controlled his body quite

differently, and he did not injure himself in such a great fall. His sister noticed immediately the new amusement which Gregor had found for himself (for as he crept around he left behind here and there traces of his sticky stuff), and so she got the idea of making Gregor's creeping around as easy as possible and thus of removing the furniture which got in the way, especially the chest of drawers and the writing desk.

But she was in no position to do this by herself. She did not dare to ask her father to help, and the servant girl would certainly not have assisted her, for although this girl, about sixteen years old, had courageously remained since the dismissal of the previous cook, she had begged for the privilege of being allowed to stay permanently confined to the kitchen and of having to open the door only in answer to a special summons. Thus, his sister had no other choice but to involve his mother while his father was absent.

His mother approached Gregor's room with cries of excited joy, but she fell silent at the door. Of course, his sister first checked whether everything in the room was in order. Only then did she let his mother walk in. In great haste Gregor had drawn the sheet down even further and wrinkled it more. The whole thing really looked just like a coverlet thrown carelessly over the couch. On this occasion, Gregor held back from spying out from under the sheet. Thus, he refrained from looking at his mother this time and was just happy that she had come.

"Come on; he is not visible," said his sister, and evidently led his mother by the hand. Now Gregor listened as these two weak women shifted the still heavy old chest of drawers from its position, and as his sister constantly took on herself the greatest part of the work, without listening to the warnings of his mother who was afraid that she would strain herself.

The work lasted a long time. After about a quarter of an hour had already gone by his mother said that it would be better if they left the chest of drawers where it was, because, in the first place, it was too heavy: they would not be finished before his father's arrival, and with the chest of drawers in the middle of the room it would block all Gregor's pathways, but, in the second place, it might not be certain that Gregor would be pleased with the removal of the furniture. To her the reverse seemed to be true; the sight of the empty walls pierced her right to the heart, and why should Gregor not feel the same, since he had been accustomed to the room furnishings for a long time and in an empty room would thus feel himself abandoned.

"And is it not the case," his mother concluded very quietly, almost whispering as if she wished to prevent Gregor, whose exact location she really didn't know, from hearing even the sound of her voice (for she was convinced that he did not understand her words), "and isn't it a fact that by removing the furniture we're showing that we're giving up all hope of an improvement and are leaving him to his own resources without any consideration? I think it would be best if we tried to keep the room exactly in the condition in which it was before, so that, when Gregor returns to us, he finds everything unchanged and can forget the intervening time all the more easily."

As he heard his mother's words Gregor realized that the lack of all immediate human contact, together with the monotonous life surrounded by the family over the course of these two months must have confused his understanding, because otherwise he couldn't explain to himself that he in all seriousness could've been so keen to have his room emptied. Was he really eager to let the warm room, comfortably furnished with pieces he had inherited, be turned into a cavern in which he would, of course, then be able to crawl about in all directions without disturbance, but at the same time with a quick and complete forgetting of his human past as well? Was he then at this point already on the verge of forgetting and was it only the voice of his mother, which he had not heard for along time, that had aroused him? Nothing was to be removed; everything must remain. In his condition he couldn't function without the beneficial influences of his furniture. And if the furniture prevented him from carrying out his senseless crawling about all over the place, then there was no harm in that, but rather a great benefit.

But his sister unfortunately thought otherwise. She had grown accustomed, certainly not without justification, so far as the discussion of matters concerning Gregor was concerned, to act as an special expert with respect to their parents, and so now the mother's advice was for his sister sufficient reason to insist on the removal, not only of the chest of drawers and the writing desk, which were the only items she had thought about at first, but also of all the furniture, with the exception of the indispensable couch. Of course, it was not only childish defiance and her recent very unexpected and hard won self-confidence which led her to this demand. She had also actually observed that Gregor needed a great deal of room to creep about; the furniture, on the other hand, as far as one could see, was not of the slightest use. But perhaps the enthusiastic sensibility of young women of her age also played a role. This feeling sought release at every opportunity, and with it Grete now felt tempted to want to make Gregor's situation even more terrifying, so that then she would be able to do even more for him than now. For surely no one except Grete would ever trust themselves to enter a room in which Gregor ruled the empty walls all by himself.

And so she did not let herself be dissuaded from her decision by her mother, who in this room seemed uncertain of herself in her sheer agitation and soon kept quiet, helping his sister with all her energy to get the chest of drawers out of the room. Now, Gregor could still do without the chest of drawers if need be, but the writing desk really had to stay. And scarcely had the women left the room with the chest of drawers, groaning as they pushed it, when Gregor stuck his head out from under the sofa to take a look how he could intervene cautiously and with as much consideration as possible. But unfortunately it was his mother who came back into the room first, while Grete had her arms wrapped around the chest of drawers in the next room and was rocking it back and forth by herself, without moving it from its position. His mother was not used to the sight of Gregor; he could have made her ill, and so, frightened, Gregor scurried backwards right to the other end of the sofa, but he could no longer prevent the sheet from moving forward a little. That was enough to catch his mother's attention. She came to a halt, stood still for a moment, and then went back to Grete.

Although Gregor kept repeating to himself over and over that really nothing unusual was going on, that only a few pieces of furniture were being rearranged, he soon had to admit to himself that the movements of the women to and fro, their quiet conversations, the scratching of the furniture on the floor affected him like a great swollen commotion on all sides, and, so firmly was he pulling in his head and legs and pressing his body into the floor, he had to tell himself unequivocally that he wouldn't be able to endure all this much longer. They were cleaning out his room, taking away from him everything he cherished; they had already dragged out the chest of drawers in which the fret saw and other tools were kept, and they were now loosening the writing desk which was fixed tight to the floor, the desk on which he, as a business student, a school student, indeed even as an elementary school student, had written out his assignments. At that moment he really didn't have any more time to check the good intentions of the two women, whose existence he had in any case almost forgotten, because in their exhaustion they were working really silently, and the heavy stumbling of their feet was the only sound to be heard.

And so he scuttled out (the women were just propping themselves up on the writing desk in the next room in order to take a breather) changing the direction of his path four times. He really didn't know what he should rescue first. Then he saw hanging conspicuously on the wall, which was otherwise already empty, the picture of the woman dressed in nothing but fur. He quickly scurried up over it and pressed himself against the glass that held it in place and which made his hot abdomen feel good. At least this picture, which Gregor at the moment completely concealed, surely no one would now take away. He twisted his head towards the door of the living room to observe the women as they came back in.

They had not allowed themselves very much rest and were coming back right away. Grete had placed her arm around her mother and held her tightly. "So what shall we take now?" said Grete and looked around her. Then her glance crossed with Gregor's from the wall. She kept her composure only because her mother was there. She bent her face towards her mother in order to prevent her from looking around, and said, although in a trembling voice and too quickly, "Come, wouldn't it be better to go back to the living room for just another moment?" Grete's purpose was clear to Gregor: she wanted to bring his mother to a safe place and then chase him down from the wall. Well, let her just attempt that! He squatted on his picture and did not hand it over. He would sooner spring into Grete's face.

But Grete's words had immediately made the mother very uneasy. She walked to the side, caught sight of the enormous brown splotch on the flowered wallpaper, and, before she became truly aware that what she was looking at was Gregor, screamed out in a high pitched raw voice "Oh God, oh God" and fell with outstretched arms, as if she was surrendering everything, down onto the couch and lay there motionless. "Gregor, you···," cried out his sister with a raised fist and an urgent glare. Since his transformation those were the first words which she had directed right at him. She ran into the room next door to

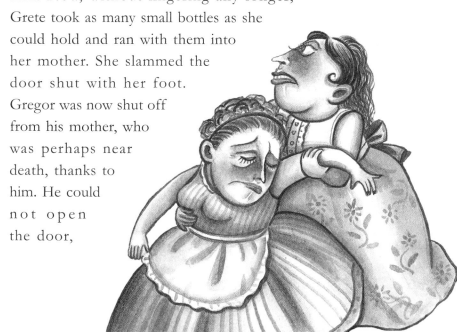

bring some spirits or other with which she could revive her mother from her fainting spell. Gregor wanted to help as well (there was time enough to save the picture), but he was stuck fast on the glass and had to tear himself loose forcefully. Then he also scurried into the next room, as if he could give his sister some advice, as in earlier times, but then he had to stand there idly behind her, while she rummaged about among various small bottles. Still, she was frightened when she turned around. A bottle fell onto the floor and shattered. A splinter of glass wounded Gregor in the face, some corrosive medicine or other dripped over him. Now, without lingering any longer, Grete took as many small bottles as she could hold and ran with them into her mother. She slammed the door shut with her foot. Gregor was now shut off from his mother, who was perhaps near death, thanks to him. He could not open the door, and he did not want to chase away his sister who had to remain with her mother. At this point he had nothing to do but wait, and overwhelmed with self-reproach and worry, he began to creep and crawl over everything: walls, furniture, and ceiling. Finally, in his despair, as the entire room started to spin around him, he fell onto the middle of the large table.

A short time elapsed. Gregor lay there limply. All around was still. Perhaps that was a good sign. Then there was ring at the door. The servant girl was naturally shut up in her kitchen, and Grete must therefore go to open the door. The father had arrived.

"What's happened," were his first words. Grete's appearance had told him everything.

Grete replied with a dull voice; evidently she was pressing her face into her father's chest: "Mother fainted, but she's getting better now. Gregor has broken loose."

"Yes, I have expected that," said his father, "I always told you that, but you women don't want to listen."

It was clear to Gregor that his father had badly misunderstood Grete's short message and was assuming that Gregor had committed some violent crime or other. Thus, Gregor now had to find his father to calm him down, for he had neither the time nor the opportunity to clarify things for him. And so he rushed away to the door of his room and pushed himself against it, so that his father could see right away as he entered from the hall that Gregor fully intended to return at once to his room, that it was not necessary to drive him back, but that one only needed to open the door and he would disappear immediately.

But his father was not in the mood to observe such niceties. "Ah," he yelled as soon as he entered, with a tone as if he were all at once angry and pleased. Gregor pulled his head back from the door and raised it in the direction of his father. He had not really pictured his father as he now stood there.

Of course, what with his new style of creeping all around, he had in the past while neglected to pay attention to what was going on in the rest of the apartment, as he had done before, and really should have grasped the fact that he would encounter different conditions. Nevertheless, nevertheless, was that still his father? Was that the same man who had lain exhausted and buried in bed in earlier days when Gregor was setting out on a business trip, who had received him on the evenings of his return in a sleeping gown and arm chair, totally incapable of standing up, who had only lifted his arm as a sign of happiness, and who in their rare strolls together a few Sundays a year and on the important holidays made his way slowly forwards between Gregor and his mother (who themselves moved slowly), always a bit more slowly than them, bundled up in his old coat, all the time setting down his walking stick carefully,

and who, when he had wanted to say something, almost always stood still and gathered his entourage around him?

But now he was standing up really straight, dressed in a tight fitting blue uniform with gold buttons, like the ones servants wear in a banking company. Above the high stiff collar of his jacket his firm double chin stuck out prominently, beneath his bushy eyebrows the glance of his black eyes was freshly penetrating and alert, his otherwise disheveled white hair was combed down into a carefully exact shining part. He threw his cap, on which a gold monogram (apparently the symbol of the bank) was affixed, in an arc across the entire room onto the sofa and moved, throwing back the edge of the long coat of his uniform, with his hands in his trouser pockets and a grim face, right up to Gregor.

He really didn't know what he had in mind, but he raised his foot uncommonly high anyway, and Gregor was astonished at the gigantic size of his sole of his boot. However, he did not linger on that point. For he knew from the first day of his new life that as far as he was concerned his father considered the greatest force the only appropriate response.

And so he scurried away from his father, stopped when his father remained standing, and scampered forward again when his father merely stirred. In this way they made their way around the room repeatedly, without anything decisive taking place; indeed because of the slow pace it didn't look like a chase. Gregor remained on the floor for the time being, especially as he was afraid that his father could take a flight up onto the wall or the ceiling as an act of real malice. At any event Gregor had to tell himself that he couldn't keep up this running around for a long time, because whenever his father took a single step, he had to go through an enormous number of movements. Already he was starting to suffer from a shortage of breath, just as in his earlier days his lungs had been quite unreliable.

As he now staggered around in this way in order to gather all his energies for running, hardly keeping his eyes open, in his listlessness he had no notion at all of any escape other than by running and had almost already forgotten that the walls were available to him, although they were obstructed by carefully carved furniture full of sharp points and

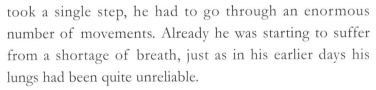

spikes—at that moment something or other thrown casually flew down close by and rolled in front of him. It was an apple; immediately a second one flew after it. Gregor stood still in fright. Further flight was useless, for his father had decided to bombard him.

From the fruit bowl on the sideboard his father had filled his pockets, and now, without for the moment taking accurate aim, was throwing apple after apple. These small red apples rolled as if electrified around on the floor and collided with each other. A weakly thrown apple grazed Gregor's back but skidded off harmlessly. However another thrown immediately after that one drove into Gregor's back really hard.

Gregor wanted to drag himself off, as if the unexpected and incredible pain would go away if he changed his position. But he felt as if he was nailed in place and lay stretched out completely confused in all his senses. Only with his final glance did he notice how the door of his room was pulled open and how, right in front of his sister (who was yelling), his mother ran out in her undergarments, for his sister had undressed her in order to give her some freedom to breathe in her fainting spell, and how his mother then ran up to his father, on the way her tied up skirts one after the other slipped toward the floor, and how, tripping over her skirts, she hurled herself onto his father and, throwing her arms around him, in complete union with him—but at this moment Gregor's powers of sight gave way—as her hands reached to the back of his father's head and she begged him to spare Gregor's life.

CHAPTER III

Gregor's serious wound, from which he suffered for over a month (since no one ventured to remove the apple, it remained in his flesh as a visible reminder), seemed by itself to have reminded the father that, in spite of his present unhappy and hateful appearance, Gregor was a member of the family, something one should not treat as an enemy, and that it was, on the contrary, a requirement of family duty to suppress one's aversion and to endure— nothing else, just endure.

And if through his wound Gregor had now apparently lost for good his ability to move and for the time being needed many many minutes to crawl across this room, like an aged invalid (so far as creeping up high was concerned, that was unimaginable), nevertheless for this worsening of his condition, in his opinion, he did get completely satisfactory compensation, because every day towards evening the door to the living room, which he was in the habit of keeping a sharp eye on even one or two hours beforehand, was opened, so that he, lying down in the darkness of his room, invisible from the living room, could see the entire family at the illuminated table and listen to their conversation, to a certain extent with their common permission, a situation quite different from what happened before.

Of course, it was no longer the animated social interaction of former times, about which Gregor in small hotel rooms had always thought about with a certain longing, when, tired out, he had to throw himself in the damp bedclothes. For the most part what went on now was very quiet. After the evening meal the father fell asleep quickly in his arm chair; the mother and sister talked guardedly to each other in the stillness. Bent far over, the mother sewed fine undergarments for a fashion shop. The sister, who had taken on a job as a salesgirl, in the evening studied stenography and French, so as perhaps later to obtain a better position. Sometimes the father woke up and, as if he was quite ignorant that he had been asleep, said to the mother "How long you have been sewing today!" and went right back to sleep, while the mother and the sister smiled tiredly to each other.

With a sort of stubbornness the father refused to take off his servant's uniform even at home, and while his sleeping gown hung unused on the coat hook, the father dozed completely dressed in his place, as if he was always ready for his responsibility and even here was waiting for the voice of his superior. As result, in spite of all the care of the mother and sister, his uniform, which even at the start was not new, grew dirty, and Gregor looked, often for the entire evening, at this clothing, with stains all over it and with its gold buttons always polished, in which the old man, although very uncomfortable, slept peacefully nonetheless.

As soon as the clock struck ten, the mother tried encouraging the father gently to wake up and then persuading him to go to bed, on the ground that he couldn't get a proper sleep here and the father, who had to report for service at six o'clock, really needed a good sleep. But in his stubbornness, which had gripped him since he had become a servant, he insisted always on staying even longer by the table, although he regularly fell asleep and then could only be prevailed upon with the greatest difficulty to trade his chair for the bed. No matter how much the mother and sister might at that point work on him with small admonitions, for a quarter of an hour he would remain shaking his head slowly, his eyes closed, without standing up. The mother would pull him by the sleeve and speak flattering words into his ear; the sister would leave her work to help her mother, but that would not have the desired effect on the father. He would settle himself even more deeply in his arm chair. Only when the two women grabbed him under the armpits would he throw his eyes open, look back and forth at the mother and sister, and habitually say "This is a life. This is the peace and quiet of my old age." And propped up by both women, he would heave himself up, elaborately, as if for him it was the greatest travail, allow himself to be led to the door by the women, wave them away there, and proceed on his own from there, while the mother quickly threw down her sewing implements and the sister her pen in order to run after the father and help him some more.

In this overworked and exhausted family who had time to worry any longer about Gregor more than was absolutely necessary? The household was constantly getting smaller. The servant girl was now let go. A huge bony cleaning woman with white hair flapping all over her head came in the morning and the evening to do the heaviest work. The mother took care of everything else in addition to her considerable sewing work. It even happened that various pieces of family jewelry, which previously the mother and sister had been overjoyed to wear on social and festive occasions, were sold, as Gregor found out in the evening from the general discussion of the prices they had fetched. But the greatest complaint was always that they could not leave this apartment, which was too big for their present means, since it was impossible to imagine how Gregor might be moved. But Gregor fully recognized that it was not just consideration for him which was preventing a move (for he could have been transported easily in a suitable box with a few air holes); the main thing holding the family back from a change in living quarters was far more their complete hopelessness and the idea that they had been struck by a misfortune like no one else in their entire circle of relatives and acquaintances.

What the world demands of poor people they now carried out to an extreme degree. The father bought breakfast to the petty officials at the bank, the mother sacrificed herself for the undergarments of strangers, the sister behind her desk was at the beck and call of customers, but the family's energies did not extend any further.

And the wound in his back began to pain Gregor all over again, when now mother and sister, after they had escorted the father to bed, came back, let their work lie, moved close together, and sat cheek to cheek and when his mother would now say, pointing to Gregor's room, "Close the door, Grete," and when Gregor was again in the darkness, while close by the women mingled their tears or, quite dry eyed, stared at the table.

Gregor spent his nights and days with hardly any sleep. Sometimes he thought that the next time the door opened he would take over the family arrangements just as he had earlier. In his imagination appeared again, after a long time, his employer and supervisor and the apprentices, the

CHAPTER III

excessively gormless custodian, two or three friends from other businesses, a chambermaid from a hotel in the provinces, a loving fleeting memory, a female cashier from a hat shop, whom he had seriously, but too slowly courted—they all appeared mixed in with strangers or people he had already forgotten, but instead of helping him and his family, they were all unapproachable, and he was happy to see them disappear.

But then he was in no mood to worry about his family. He was filled with sheer anger over the wretched care he was getting, even though he couldn't imagine anything for which he might have an appetite. Still, he made plans about how he could take from the larder what he at all account deserved, even if he wasn't hungry. Without thinking any more about how one might be able to give Gregor special pleasure, the sister now kicked some food or other very quickly into his room in the morning and at noon, before she ran off to her shop, and in the evening, quite indifferent about whether the food had perhaps only been tasted or, what happened most frequently, remained entirely undisturbed, she whisked it out with one sweep of her broom. The task of cleaning his room, which she now always carried out in the evening, could not be done any more quickly.

Streaks of dirt ran along the walls; here and there lay tangles of dust and garbage. At first, when his sister arrived, Gregor positioned himself in a particularly filthy corner in order with this posture to make something of a protest. But he could have well stayed there for weeks without his sister's changing her ways. Indeed, she perceived the dirt as much as he did, but she had decided just to let it stay. In this business, with a touchiness which was quite new to her and which had generally taken over the entire family, she kept watch to see that the cleaning of Gregor's room remained reserved for her.

Once his mother had undertaken a major cleaning of Gregor's room, which she had only completed successfully after using a few buckets of water. But the extensive dampness made Gregor sick and he lay supine, embittered and immobile on the couch. However, the mother's punishment was not delayed for long. For in the evening the sister had hardly observed the change in Gregor's room before she ran into the living room mightily offended and, in spite of her mother's hand lifted high in entreaty, broke out in a fit of crying. Her parents (the father had, of course, woken up with a start in his arm chair) at first looked at her astonished and helpless; until they started to get agitated. Turning to his right, the father heaped reproaches on the mother that she was not to take over the cleaning of Gregor's room from the sister and, turning to his left, he shouted at the sister that she would no longer be allowed to clean Gregor's room ever again, while the mother tried to pull the father, beside himself in his excitement, into the bed room; the sister, shaken by her crying fit, pounded on the table with her tiny fists, and Gregor hissed at all this, angry that no one thought about shutting the door and sparing him the sight of this commotion.

But even when the sister, exhausted from her daily work, had grown tired of caring for Gregor as she had before, even then the mother did not have to come at all on her behalf. And Gregor did not have to be neglected. For now the cleaning woman was there. This old widow, who in her long life must have managed to survive the worst with the help of her bony frame, had no real horror of Gregor. Without being in the least curious, she had once by chance opened Gregor's door. At the sight of Gregor, who, totally surprised, began to scamper here and there, although no one was chasing him, she remained standing with her hands folded across her stomach staring at him. Since then she did not fail to open the door furtively a little every morning and evening to look in on Gregor. At first, she also called him to her with words which she presumably thought were friendly, like "Come here for a bit, old dung beetle!" or "Hey, look at the old dung beetle!" Addressed in such a manner, Gregor answered nothing, but remained motionless in his place, as if the door had not been opened at all.

If only, instead of allowing this cleaning woman to disturb him uselessly whenever she felt like it, they had instead given her orders to clean up his room every day! One day in the early morning (a hard downpour, perhaps already a sign of the coming spring, struck the window panes) when the cleaning woman started up once again with her usual conversation, Gregor was so bitter that he turned towards her, as if for an attack, although slowly and weakly. But instead of being afraid of him, the cleaning woman merely lifted up a chair standing close by the door and, as she stood there with her mouth wide open, her intention was clear: she would close her mouth only when the chair in her hand had been thrown down on Gregor's back. "This goes no further, all right?" she asked, as Gregor turned himself around again, and she placed the chair calmly back in the corner.

Gregor ate hardly anything any more. Only when he chanced to move past the food which had been prepared did he, as a game, take a bit into his mouth, hold it there for hours, and generally spit it out again. At first he thought it might be his sadness over the condition of his room which kept him from eating, but he very soon became reconciled to the alterations in his room. People had grown accustomed to put into storage in his room things which they couldn't put anywhere else, and at this point there were many such things, now that they had rented one room of the apartment to three lodgers. These solemn gentlemen (all three had full beards, as Gregor once found out through a crack in the door) were meticulously intent on tidiness, not only in their own room but (since they had now rented a room here) in the entire household, and particularly in the kitchen. They simply did not tolerate any useless or shoddy stuff.

Moreover, for the most part they had brought with them their own pieces of furniture. Thus, many items had become superfluous, and these were not really things one could sell or things people wanted to throw out. All these items ended up in Gregor's room, even the box of ashes and the garbage pail from the kitchen. The cleaning woman, always in a hurry, simply flung anything that was momentarily useless into Gregor's room. Fortunately Gregor generally saw only the relevant object and the hand which held it. The cleaning woman perhaps was intending, when time and opportunity allowed, to take the stuff out again or to throw everything out all at once, but in fact the things remained lying there, wherever they had ended up at the first throw, unless Gregor squirmed his way through the accumulation of junk and moved it. At first he was forced to do this because otherwise there was no room for him to creep around, but later he did it with a growing pleasure, although after such movements, tired to death and feeling wretched, he didn't budge for hours.

Because the lodgers sometimes also took their evening meal at home in the common living room, the door to the living room stayed shut on many evenings. But Gregor had no trouble at all going without the open door. Already on many evenings when it was open he had not availed himself of it, but, without the family noticing, was stretched out in the darkest corner of his room. However, once the cleaning woman had left the door to the living room slightly ajar, and it remained open even when the lodgers came in in the evening and the lights were put on. They sat down at the head of the table, where in earlier days the mother, the father, and Gregor had eaten, unfolded their serviettes, and picked up their knives and forks. The mother immediately appeared in the door with a dish of meat and right behind her the sister with a dish piled high with potatoes. The food gave off a lot of steam. The gentlemen lodgers bent over the plate set before them, as if they wanted to check it before eating, and in fact the one who sat in the middle (for the other two he seemed to serve as the authority) cut off a piece of meat still on the plate obviously to establish whether it was sufficiently tender and whether or not something should be shipped back to the kitchen. He was satisfied, and mother and sister, who had looked on in suspense, began to breathe easily and to smile.

The family itself ate in the kitchen. In spite of that,

before the father went into the kitchen, he came into the room and with a single bow, cap in hand, made a tour of the table. The lodgers rose up collectively and murmured something in their beards. Then, when they were alone, they ate almost in complete silence. It seemed odd to Gregor that out of all the many different sorts of sounds of eating, what was always audible was their chewing teeth, as if by that Gregor should be shown that people needed their teeth to eat and that nothing could be done even with the most handsome toothless jawbone.

"I really do have an appetite," Gregor said to himself sorrowfully, "but not for these things. How these lodgers stuff themselves, and I am dying."

On this very evening (Gregor didn't remember hearing the violin all through this period) it sounded from the kitchen. The lodgers had already ended their night meal, the middle one had pulled out a newspaper and had given each of the other two a page, and they were now leaning back, reading and smoking. When the violin started playing, they became attentive, got up, and went on tiptoe to the hall door, at which they remained standing pressed up against one another.

They must have been audible from the kitchen, because the father called out "Perhaps the gentlemen don't like the playing? It can be stopped at once."

"On the contrary," stated the lodger in the middle,

"might the young woman not come into us and play in the room here where it is really much more comfortable and cheerful?"

"Oh, thank you," cried out the father, as if he were the one playing the violin.

The men stepped back into the room and waited. Soon the father came with the music stand, the mother with the sheet music, and the sister with the violin. The sister calmly prepared everything for the recital. The parents, who had never previously rented a room and therefore exaggerated their politeness to the lodgers, dared not sit on their own chairs. The father leaned against the door, his right hand stuck between two buttons of his buttoned up uniform. The mother, however, accepted a chair offered by one lodger. Since she left the chair sit where the gentleman had chanced to put it, she sat to one side in a corner.

The sister began to play. The father and mother, followed attentively, one on each side, the movements of her hands. Attracted by the playing, Gregor had ventured to advance a little further forward and his head was already in the living room. He scarcely wondered about the fact that recently he had had so little consideration for the others; earlier this consideration had been something he was proud of. And for that very reason he would've had at this moment more reason to hide away, because as a result of the dust which lay all over his room and flew around with the slightest movement, he was totally covered in dirt. On his back and his sides he carted around with him dust, threads, hair, and remnants of food. His indifference to everything was much too great for him to lie on his back and scour himself on the carpet, as he often had done earlier during the day. In spite of his condition he had no timidity about inching forward a bit on the spotless floor of the living room.

In any case, no one paid him any attention. The family was all caught up in the violin playing. The lodgers, by contrast, who for the moment had placed themselves, their hands in their trouser pockets, behind the music stand much too close to the sister, so that they could all see the sheet music, something that must certainly bother the sister, soon drew back to the window conversing in low voices with bowed heads, where they then remained, worriedly observed by the father. It now seemed really clear that, having assumed they were to hear a beautiful or entertaining violin recital, they were disappointed, and were allowing their peace and quiet to be disturbed only out of politeness. The way in which they all blew the smoke from their cigars out of their noses and mouths in particular led one to conclude that they were very irritated. And yet his sister was playing so beautifully. Her face was turned to the side, her gaze followed the score intently and sadly.

Gregor crept forward still a little further and kept his

head close against the floor in order to be able to catch her gaze if possible. Was he an animal that music so seized him? For him it was as if the way to the unknown nourishment he craved was revealing itself to him. He was determined to press forward right to his sister, to tug at her dress and to indicate to her in this way that she might still come with her violin into his room, because here no one valued the recital as he wanted to value it. He did not wish to let her go from his room any more, at least not as long as he lived. His frightening appearance would for the first time become useful for him. He wanted to be at all the doors of his room simultaneously and snarl back at the attackers. However, his sister should not be compelled but would remain with him voluntarily; she would sit next to him on the sofa, bend down her ear to him, and he would then confide in her that he firmly intended to send her to the conservatory and that, if his misfortune had not arrived in the interim, he would have declared all this last Christmas (had Christmas really already come and gone?), and would have brooked no argument. After this explanation his sister would break out in tears of emotion, and Gregor would lift himself up to her armpit and kiss her throat, which she, from the time she started going to work, had left exposed without a band or a collar.

"Mr. Samsa," called out the middle lodger to the father, and pointed his index finger, without uttering a further word, at Gregor as he was moving slowly forward. The violin fell silent. The middle lodger smiled, first shaking his head once at his friends, and then looked down at Gregor once more. Rather than driving Gregor back again, the father seemed to consider it of prime importance to calm down the lodgers, although they were not at all upset and Gregor seemed to entertain them more than the violin recital.

The father hurried over to them and with outstretched arms tried to push them into their own room and simultaneously to block their view of Gregor with his own body. At this point they became really somewhat irritated, although one no longer knew whether that was because of the father's behaviour or because of knowledge they had just acquired that they had had, without knowing it, a neighbour like Gregor. They demanded explanations from his father, raised their arms to make their points, tugged agitatedly at their beards, and moved back towards their room quite slowly. In the meantime, the isolation which had suddenly fallen upon his sister after the sudden breaking off of the recital had overwhelmed her. She had held onto the violin and bow in her limp hands for a little while and had continued to look at the sheet music as if she was still playing. All at once she pulled herself together, placed the instrument in her mother's lap (the mother was still sitting in her chair having trouble breathing and with her lungs labouring) and had run into the next room, which the lodgers, pressured by the father, were already approaching more rapidly. One could observe how under the sister's practiced hands the sheets and pillows on the beds were thrown on high and arranged. Even before the lodgers had reached the room, she was finished fixing the beds and was slipping out.

The father seemed so gripped once again with his

stubbornness that he forgot about the respect which he always owed to his renters. He pressed on and on, until at the door of the room the middle gentleman stamped loudly with his foot and thus brought the father to a standstill.

"I hereby declare," the middle lodger said, raising his hand and casting his glance both on the mother and the sister, "that considering the disgraceful conditions prevailing in this apartment and family," with this he spat decisively on the floor, "I immediately cancel my room. I will, of course, pay nothing at all for the days which I have lived here; on the contrary I shall think about whether or not I will initiate some sort of action against you, something which—believe me— will be very easy to establish." He fell silent and looked directly in front of him, as if he was waiting for something. In fact, his two friends immediately joined in with their opinions, "We also give immediate notice." At that he seized the door handle, banged the door shut, and locked it.

The father groped his way tottering to his chair and let himself fall in it. It looked as if he was stretching out for his usual evening snooze, but the heavy nodding of his head (which looked as if it was without support) showed that he was not sleeping at all. Gregor had lain motionless the entire time in the spot where the lodgers had caught him. Disappointment with the collapse of his plan and perhaps also his weakness brought on his severe hunger made it impossible for him to move. He was certainly afraid that a general disaster would break over him at any moment, and he waited. He was not even startled when the violin fell from the mother's lap, out from under her trembling fingers, and gave off a reverberating tone.

"My dear parents," said the sister banging her hand on the table by way of an introduction, "things cannot go on any longer in this way. Maybe if you don't understand that, well, I do. I will not utter my brother's name in front of this monster, and thus I say only that we must try to get rid of it. We have tried what is humanly possible to take care of it and to be patient. I believe that no one can criticize us in the slightest."

"She is right in a thousand ways," said the father to himself. The mother, who was still incapable of breathing properly, began to cough numbly with her hand held up over her mouth and a manic expression in her eyes.

The sister hurried over to her mother and held her forehead. The sister's words seemed to have led the father to certain reflections. He sat upright, played with his uniform hat among the plates, which still lay on the table from the lodgers' evening meal, and looked now and then at the motionless Gregor.

"We must try to get rid of it," the sister now said decisively to the father, for the mother, in her coughing fit, wasn't listening to anything, "it is killing you both. I see it coming. When people have to work as hard as we all do, they cannot also tolerate this endless torment at home. I just can't go on any more." And she broke out into such a crying fit that her tears flowed out down onto her mother's face. She wiped them off her mother with mechanical motions of her hands.

"Child," said the father sympathetically and with obvious appreciation, "then what should we do?"

The sister only shrugged her shoulders as a sign of the perplexity which, in contrast to her previous confidence, had come over her while she was crying.

"If only he understood us," said the father in a semi-questioning tone. The sister, in the midst of her sobbing, shook her hand energetically as a sign that there was no point thinking of that.

"If he only understood us," repeated the father and by shutting his eyes he absorbed the sister's conviction of the impossibility of this point, "then perhaps some compromise would be possible with him. But as it is···"

"It must be gotten rid of," cried the sister; "That is the only way, father. You must try to get rid of the idea that this is Gregor. The fact that we have believed for so long, that is truly our real misfortune. But how can it be Gregor? If it were Gregor, he would have long ago realized that a communal life among human beings is not possible with such an animal and would have gone away voluntarily. Then we would not have a brother, but we could go on living and honour his memory. But this animal plagues us. It drives away the lodgers, will obviously take over the entire apartment, and leave us to spend the night in the alley. Just look, father," she suddenly cried out, "he's already starting up again."

With a fright which was totally incomprehensible to Gregor, the sister even left the mother, pushed herself away from her chair, as if she would sooner sacrifice her mother than remain in Gregor's vicinity, and rushed behind her father who, excited merely by her behaviour, also stood up and half raised his arms in front of the sister as though to protect her.

But Gregor did not have any notion of wishing to create problems for anyone and certainly not for his sister. He had just started to turn himself around in order to creep back into his room, quite a startling sight, since, as a result of his suffering condition, he had to guide himself through the difficulty of turning around with his head, in this process lifting and banging it against the floor several times. He paused and looked around. His good intentions seem to have been recognized. The fright had only lasted for a moment. Now they looked at him in silence and sorrow. His mother lay in her chair, with her legs stretched out and pressed together; her eyes were almost shut from weariness. The father and sister sat next to one another.

The sister had set her hands around the father's neck.

"Now perhaps I can actually turn myself around," thought Gregor and began the task again. He couldn't stop puffing at the effort and had to rest now and then.

Besides no on was urging him on. It was all left to him on his own. When he had completed turning around, he immediately began to wander straight back. He was astonished at the great distance which separated him from his room and did not understand in the least how in his weakness he had covered the same distance a short time before, almost without noticing it. Constantly intent only on creeping along quickly, he hardly paid any attention to the fact that no word or cry from his family interrupted him.

Only when he was already in the door did he turn his head, not completely, because he felt his neck growing stiff. At any rate he still saw that behind him nothing had changed. Only the sister was standing up. His last glimpse brushed over the mother who was now completely asleep. Hardly was he inside his room when the door was pushed shut very quickly, bolted fast, and barred.

Gregor was startled by the sudden commotion behind him, so much so that his little limbs bent double under him. It was his sister who had been in such a hurry. She had stood up right away, had waited, and had then sprung forward nimbly. Gregor had not heard anything of her approach. She cried out "Finally!" to her parents, as she turned the key in the lock.

"What now?" Gregor asked himself and looked around him in the darkness. He soon made the discovery that he could no longer move at all. He was not surprised at that. On the contrary, it struck him as unnatural that he had really been able up to this point to move around with these thin little legs. Besides he felt relatively content. True, he had pains throughout his entire body, but it seemed to him that they were gradually becoming weaker and weaker and would finally go away completely. The rotten apple in his back and the inflamed surrounding area, entirely covered with white dust, he hardly noticed. He remembered his family with deep feeling and love. In this business, his own thought that he had to disappear was, if possible, even more decisive than his sister's. He remained in this state of empty and peaceful reflection until the tower clock struck three o'clock in the morning. From the window he witnessed the beginning of the general dawning outside. Then without willing it, his head sank all the way down, and from his nostrils flowed out weakly out his last breath.

Early in the morning the cleaning woman came. In her sheer energy and haste she banged all the doors (in precisely the way people had already asked her to avoid), so much so that once she arrived a quiet sleep was no longer possible anywhere in the entire apartment. In her customarily brief visit to Gregor she at first found nothing special. She thought he lay so immobile there intending to play the offended party. She gave him credit for as complete an understanding as possible. Because she happened to hold the long broom in her hand, she tried to tickle Gregor with it from the door. When that was quite unsuccessful, she became irritated and poked Gregor a little, and only when she had shoved him from his place without any resistance did she become attentive. When she quickly realized the true state of affairs, her eyes grew large, she whistled to herself, but didn't restrain herself for long. She pulled open the door of the bedroom and yelled in a loud voice into the darkness, "Come and look. It's kicked the bucket. It's lying there, totally snuffed!"

The Samsa married couple sat upright in their marriage bed and had to get over their fright at the cleaning woman before they managed to grasp her message. But then Mr. and Mrs. Samsa climbed very quickly out of bed, one on either side. Mr. Samsa threw the bedspread over his shoulders, Mrs. Samsa came out only in her night-shirt, and like this they stepped into Gregor's room. Meanwhile the door of the living room (in which Grete had slept since the lodgers had arrived on the scene) had also opened. She was fully clothed, as if she had not slept at all; her white face also seem to indicate that.

"Dead?" said Mrs. Samsa and looked questioningly

at the cleaning woman, although she could check everything on her own and even understand without a check.

"I should say so," said the cleaning woman and, by way of proof, poked Gregor's body with the broom a considerable distance more to the side. Mrs. Samsa made a movement as if she wished to restrain the broom, but didn't do it.

"Well," said Mr. Samsa, "now we can give thanks to God." He crossed himself, and the three women followed his example.

Grete, who did not take her eyes off the corpse, said, "Look how thin he was. He had eaten nothing for such a long time. The meals which came in here came out again exactly the same."

In fact, Gregor's body was completely flat and dry. That was apparent really for the first time, now that he was no longer raised on his small limbs and, moreover, now that nothing else distracted one's gaze.

"Grete, come into us for a moment," said Mrs. Samsa with a melancholy smile, and Grete went, not without looking back at the corpse, behind her parents into the bed room. The cleaning woman shut the door and opened the window wide. In spite of the early morning, the fresh air was partly tinged with warmth. It was already the end of March.

The three lodgers stepped out of their room and looked around for their breakfast, astonished that they had been forgotten.

"Where is the breakfast?" asked the middle one of the gentlemen grumpily to the cleaning woman. However, she laid her finger to her lips and then quickly and silently indicated to the lodgers that they could come into Gregor's room. So they came and stood around Gregor's corpse, their hands in the pockets of their somewhat worn jackets, in the room, which was already quite bright.

Then the door of the bed room opened, and Mr. Samsa appeared in his uniform, with his wife on one arm and his daughter on the other. All were a little tear stained. Now and then Grete pressed her face onto her father's arm.

"Get out of my apartment immediately," said Mr. Samsa and pulled open the door, without letting go of the women.

"What do you mean?" said the middle lodger, somewhat dismayed and with a sugary smile. The two others kept their hands behind them and constantly rubbed them against each other, as if in joyful anticipation of a great squabble which must end up in their favour.

"I mean exactly what I say," replied Mr. Samsa and went directly with his two female companions up to the lodger. The latter at first stood there motionless and looked at the floor, as if matters were arranging themselves in a new way in his head.

"All right, then we'll go," he said and looked up at Mr. Samsa as if, suddenly overcome by humility, he was asking fresh permission for this decision. Mr. Samsa merely nodded to him repeatedly with his eyes open wide.

Following that, the lodger actually went immediately with long strides into the hall. His two friends had already been listening for a while with their hands quite still, and now they hopped smartly after him, as if afraid that Mr. Samsa could step into the hall ahead of them and disturb their reunion with their leader. In the hall all three of them took their hats from the coat rack, pulled their canes from the cane holder, bowed silently, and left the apartment.

In what turned out to be an entirely groundless mistrust, Mr. Samsa stepped with the two women out onto the landing, leaned against the railing, and looked down as the three lodgers slowly but steadily made their way down

CHAPTER III

the long staircase, disappeared on each floor in a certain turn of the stairwell and in a few seconds came out again. The deeper they proceeded, the more the Samsa family lost interest in them, and when a butcher with a tray on his head come to meet them and then with a proud bearing ascended the stairs high above them, Mr. Samsa., together with the women, left the banister, and they all returned, as if relieved, back into their apartment.

They decided to pass that day resting and going for a stroll. Not only had they earned this break from work, but there was no question that they really needed it. And so they sat down at the table and wrote three letters of apology: Mr. Samsa to his supervisor, Mrs. Samsa to her client, and Grete to her proprietor. During the writing the cleaning woman came in to say that she was going off, for her morning work was finished. The three people writing at first merely nodded, without glancing up. Only when the cleaning woman was still unwilling to depart, did they look up angrily.

"Well?" asked Mr. Samsa.

The cleaning woman stood smiling in the doorway, as if she had a great stroke of luck to report to the family but would only do it if she was asked directly. The almost upright small ostrich feather in her hat, which had irritated Mr. Samsa during her entire service, swayed lightly in all directions.

"All right then, what do you really want?" asked Mrs. Samsa, whom the cleaning lady still usually respected.

"Well," answered the cleaning woman (smiling so happily she couldn't go on speaking right away), "about how that rubbish from the next room should be thrown out, you mustn't worry about it. It's all taken care of."

Mrs. Samsa and Grete bent down to their letters, as though they wanted to go on writing; Mr. Samsa, who noticed that the cleaning woman wanted to start describing everything in detail, decisively prevented her with an outstretched hand. But since she was not allowed to explain, she remembered the great hurry she was in, and called out, clearly insulted, "Ta ta, everyone," turned around furiously and left the apartment with a fearful slamming of the door.

"This evening she'll be let go," said Mr. Samsa, but he got no answer from either his wife or from his daughter, because the cleaning woman seemed to have upset once again the tranquillity they had just attained. They got up, went to the window and remained there, with their arms about each other. Mr. Samsa turned around in his chair in their direction and observed them quietly for a while.

Then he called out, "All right, come here then. Let's finally get rid of old things. And have a little consideration for me." The women attended to him at once. They rushed to him, caressed him, and quickly ended their letters.

Then all three left the apartment together, something they had not done for months now, and took the electric tram into the open air outside the city. The car in which they were sitting by themselves was totally engulfed by the warm sun. They talked to each other, leaning back comfortably in their seats, about future prospects, and they discovered that on closer observation these were not at all bad, for all three had employment, about which they had not really questioned each other at all, which was extremely favorable and with especially promising prospects. The greatest improvement in their situation at this moment, of course, had to come from a change of dwelling. Now they wanted to rent an apartment smaller and cheaper but better situated and generally more practical than the present one, which Gregor had found. While they amused themselves in this way, it struck Mr. and Mrs. Samsa almost at the same moment how their daughter, who was getting more animated all the time, had blossomed recently, in spite of all the troubles which had made her cheeks pale, into a beautiful and voluptuous young woman. Growing more silent and almost unconsciously understanding each other in their glances, they thought that the time was now at hand to seek out a good honest man for her. And it was something of a confirmation of their new dreams and good intentions when at the end of their journey the daughter first lifted herself up and stretched her young body.

A Hungry Artist

In the last decades interest in hunger artists has declined considerably. Whereas in earlier days there was good money to be earned putting on major productions of this sort under one's own management, nowadays that is totally impossible. Those were different times. Back then the hunger artist captured the attention of the entire city. From day to day while the fasting lasted, participation increased. Everyone wanted to see the hunger artist at least daily. During the final days there were people with subscription tickets who sat all day in front of the small barred cage. And there were even viewing hours at night, their impact heightened by torchlight.

On fine days the cage was dragged out into the open air, and then the hunger artist was put on display particularly for the children. While for grown-ups the hunger artist was often merely a joke, something they participated in because it was fashionable, the children looked on amazed, their mouths open, holding each other's hands for safety, as he sat there on scattered straw — spurning a chair — in a black

tights, looking pale, with his ribs sticking out prominently, sometimes nodding politely, answering questions with a forced smile, even sticking his arm out through the bars to let people feel how emaciated he was, but then completely sinking back into himself, so that he paid no attention to anything, not even to what was so important to him, the striking of the clock, which was the single furnishing in the cage, merely looking out in front of him with his eyes almost shut and now and then sipping from a tiny glass of water to moisten his lips.

Apart from the changing groups of spectators there were also constant observers chosen by the public — strangely enough they were usually butchers — who, always three at a time, were given the task of observing the hunger artist day and night, so that he didn't get something to eat in some secret manner. It was, however, merely a formality, introduced to reassure the masses, for those who understood knew well enough that during the period of fasting the hunger artist would never, under any circumstances, have eaten the slightest thing, not even if compelled by force. The honour of his art forbade it. Naturally, none of the watchers understood that. Sometimes there were nightly groups of watchers who carried out their vigil very laxly, deliberately sitting together in a distant corner and putting all their attention into playing cards there, clearly intending to allow the hunger

artist a small refreshment, which, according to their way of thinking, he could get from some secret supplies. Nothing was more excruciating to the hunger artist than such watchers. They depressed him. They made his fasting terribly difficult. Sometimes he overcame his weakness and sang during the time they were observing, for as long as he could keep it up, to show people how unjust their suspicions about him were. But that was little help. For then they just wondered among themselves about his skill at being able to eat even while singing.

He much preferred the observers who sat down right against the bars and, not satisfied with the dim backlighting of the room, illuminated him with electric flashlights. The glaring light didn't bother him in the slightest. Generally he couldn't sleep at all, and he could always doze under any lighting and at any hour, even in an

overcrowded, noisy auditorium. With such observers, he was very happily prepared to spend the entire night without sleeping. He was very pleased to joke with them, to recount stories from his nomadic life and then, in turn, to listen their stories — doing everything just to keep them awake, so that he could keep showing them once again that he had nothing to eat in his cage and that he was fasting as none of them could.

He was happiest, however, when morning came and a lavish breakfast was brought for them at his own expense, on which they hurled themselves with the appetite of healthy men after a hard night's work without sleep. True, there were still people who wanted to see in this breakfast an unfair means of influencing the observers, but that was going too far, and if they were asked whether they wanted to undertake the observers' night shift for its own sake, without the breakfast, they excused themselves. But nonetheless they stood by their suspicions.

However, it was, in general, part of fasting that these doubts were inextricably associated with it. For, in fact, no one was in a position to spend time watching the hunger artist every day and night, so no one could know, on the basis of his own observation, whether this was a case of truly uninterrupted, flawless fasting. The hunger artist himself was the only one who could know that and, at the same time, the only spectator capable of being completely

satisfied with his own fasting. But the reason he was never satisfied was something different. Perhaps it was not fasting at all which made him so very emaciated that many people, to their own regret, had to stay away from his performance, because they couldn't bear to look at him. For he was also so skeletal out of dissatisfaction with himself, because he alone knew something that even initiates didn't know — how easy it was to fast. It was the easiest thing in the world. About this he did not remain silent, but people did not believe him. At best they thought he was being modest. Most of them, however, believed he was a publicity seeker or a total swindler, for whom, at all events, fasting was easy, because he understood how to make it easy, and then had the nerve to half admit it. He had to accept all that. Over the years he had become accustomed to it. But this dissatisfaction kept gnawing at his insides all the time and never yet — and this one had to say to his credit — had he left the cage of his own free will after any period of fasting.

The impresario had set the maximum length of time for the fast at forty days — he would never allow the fasting go on beyond that point, not even in the cosmopolitan cities. And, in fact, he had a good reason. Experience had shown that for about forty days one could increasingly whip up a city's interest by gradually increasing advertising, but that then the people turned away — one could demonstrate a significant decline in popularity. In this respect, there were,

of course, small differences among different towns and among different countries, but as a rule it was true that forty days was the maximum length of time.

So then on the fortieth day the door of the cage — which was covered with flowers — was opened, an enthusiastic audience filled the amphitheatre, a military band played, two doctors entered the cage, in order to take the necessary measurements of the hunger artist, the results were announced to the auditorium through a megaphone, and finally two young ladies arrived, happy about the fact that they were the ones who had just been selected by lot, seeking to lead the hunger artist down a couple of steps out of the cage, where on a small table a carefully chosen hospital meal was laid out. And at this moment the hunger artist always fought back. Of course, he still freely laid his bony arms in the helpful outstretched hands of the ladies bending over him, but he did not want to stand up. Why stop right now after forty days? He could have kept going for even longer, for an unlimited length of time. Why stop right now, when he was in his best form, indeed, not yet even in his best fasting form? Why did people want to rob him of the fame of fasting longer, not just so that he could become the greatest hunger artist of all time, which he probably was already, but also so that he could surpass himself in some unimaginable way, for he felt there were no limits to his capacity for fasting. Why did this

crowd, which pretended to admire him so much, have so little patience with him? If he kept going and kept fasting longer, why would they not tolerate it? Then, too, he was tired and felt good sitting in the straw. Now he was supposed to stand up straight and tall and go to eat, something which, when he just imagined it, made him feel nauseous right away. With great difficulty he repressed mentioning this only out of consideration for the women. And he looked up into the eyes of these women, apparently so friendly but in reality so cruel, and shook his excessively heavy head on his feeble neck.

But then happened what always happened. The impresario came and in silence — the music made talking impossible — raised his arms over the hunger artist, as if inviting heaven to look upon its work here on the straw, this unfortunate martyr, something the hunger artist certainly was, only in a completely different sense, then grabbed the hunger artist around his thin waist, in the process wanting with his exaggerated caution to make people believe that here he had to deal with something fragile, and handed him over — not without secretly shaking him a little, so that the hunger artist's legs and upper body swung back and forth uncontrollably — to the women, who had in the meantime turned as pale as death. At this point, the hunger artist endured everything. His head lay on his chest — it was as if it had inexplicably rolled around and just stopped there

— his body was arched back, his legs, in an impulse of self-preservation, pressed themselves together at the knees, but scraped the ground, as if they were not really on the floor but were looking for the real ground, and the entire weight of his body,  admittedly very small, lay against one of the women, who appealed for help with flustered breath, for she had not imagined her post of honour would be like this, and then stretched her neck as far as possible, to keep her face from the least contact with the hunger artist, but then, when she couldn't manage this and her more fortunate companion didn't come to her assistance but trembled and remained content to hold in front of her the hunger artist's hand, that small bundle of knuckles, she broke into tears, to the delighted laughter of the auditorium, and had to be relieved by an attendant who had been standing ready for some time. Then came the meal. The impresario put a little food into mouth of the hunger

artist, now half unconscious, as if fainting, and kept up a cheerful patter designed to divert attention away from the hunger artist's condition. Then a toast was proposed to the public, which was supposedly whispered to the impresario by the hunger artist, the orchestra confirmed everything with a great fanfare, people dispersed, and no one had the right to be dissatisfied with the event, no one except the hunger artist — he was always the only one.

He lived this way, taking small regular breaks, for many years, apparently in the spotlight, honoured by the world, but for all that his mood was usually gloomy, and it kept growing gloomier all the time, because no one understood how to take him seriously. But how was he to find consolation? What was there left for him to wish for? And if a goodnatured man who felt sorry for him ever wanted to explain to him that his sadness probably came from his fasting, then it could happen that the hunger artist responded with an outburst of rage and began to shake the bars like an animal, frightening everyone. But the impresario had a way of punishing moments like this, something he was happy to use. He would make an apology for the hunger artist to the assembled public, conceding that the irritability had been provoked only by his fasting, something quite intelligible to wellfed people and capable of excusing the behaviour of the hunger artist without further explanation. From there he would move on to

speak about the equally hard to understand claim of the hunger artist that he could go on fasting for much longer than he was doing. He would praise the lofty striving, the good will, and the great self-denial no doubt contained in this claim, but then would try to contradict it simply by producing photographs, which were also on sale, for in the pictures one could see the hunger artist on the fortieth day of his fast, in bed, almost dead from exhaustion. Although the hunger artist was very familiar with this perversion of the truth, it always strained his nerves again and was too much for him. What was a result of the premature ending of the fast people were now proposing as its cause! It was impossible to fight against this lack of understanding, against this world of misunderstanding. In good faith he always listened eagerly to the impresario at the bars of his cage, but each time, once the photographs came out, he would let go of the bars and, with a sigh, sink back into the straw, and a reassured public could come up again and view him.

When those who had witnessed such scenes thought back on them a few years later, often they were unable to understand themselves. For in the meantime that change mentioned above had set it. It happened almost immediately. There may have been more profound reasons for it, but who bothered to discover what they were? At any rate, one day the pampered hunger artist saw himself

abandoned by the crowd of pleasure seekers, who preferred to stream to other attractions. The impresario chased around half of Europe one more time with him, to see whether he could still re-discover the old interest here and there. It was all futile. It was as if a secret agreement against the fasting performances had developed everywhere. Naturally, it couldn't really have happened all at once, and people later remembered some things which in the days of intoxicating success they hadn't paid sufficient attention to, some inadequately suppressed indications, but now it was too late to do anything to counter them. Of course, it was certain that the popularity of fasting would return once more someday, but for those now alive that was no consolation. What was the hunger artist to do now? A man whom thousands of people had cheered on could not display himself in show booths at small fun fairs. The hunger artist was not only too old to take up a different profession, but was fanatically devoted to fasting more than anything else. So he said farewell to the impresario, an incomparable companion on his life's road, and let himself be hired by a large circus. In order to spare his own feelings, he didn't even look at the terms of his contract at all.

A large circus with its huge number of men, animals, and gimmicks, which are constantly being let go and replenished, can use anyone at any time, even a hunger

artist, provided, of course, his demands are modest. Moreover, in this particular case it was not only the hunger artist himself who was engaged, but also his old and famous name. In fact, given the characteristic nature of his art, which was not diminished by his advancing age, one could never claim that a worn out artist, who no longer stood at the pinnacle of his ability, wanted to escape to a quiet position in the circus. On the contrary, the hunger artist declared that he could fast just as well as in earlier times — something that was entirely credible. Indeed, he even affirmed that if people would let him do what he wanted — and he was promised this without further ado — he would really now legitimately amaze the world for the first time, an assertion which, however, given the mood of the time, which the hunger artist in his enthusiasm easily overlooked, only brought smiles from the experts.

However, basically the hunger artist had not forgotten his sense of the way things really were, and he took it as self-evident that people would not set him and his cage up as the star attraction somewhere in the middle of the arena, but would move him outside in some other readily accessible spot near the animal stalls. Huge brightly painted signs surrounded the cage and announced what there was to look at there. During the intervals in the main performance, when the general public pushed out towards the menagerie in order to see the animals, they could hardly

avoid moving past the hunger artist and stopping there a moment. They would perhaps have remained with him longer, if those pushing up behind them in the narrow passage way, who did not understand this pause on the way to the animal stalls they wanted to see, had not made a longer peaceful observation impossible. This was also the reason why the hunger artist began to tremble at these visiting hours, which he naturally used to long for as the main purpose of his life. In the early days he could hardly wait for the pauses in the performances. He had looked forward with delight to the crowd pouring around him, until he became convinced only too quickly — and even the most stubborn, almost deliberate self-deception could not hold out against the experience — that, judging by their intentions, most of these people were, again and again without exception, only visiting the menagerie. And this view from a distance still remained his most beautiful moment. For when they had come right up to him, he immediately got an earful from the shouting of the two steadily increasing groups, the ones who wanted to take their time looking at the hunger artist, not with any understanding but on a whim or from mere defiance — for him these ones were soon the more painful — and a second group of people whose only demand was to go straight to the animal stalls.

Once the large crowds had passed, the late comers

would arrive, and although there was nothing preventing these people any more from sticking around for as long as they wanted, they rushed past with long strides, almost without a sideways glance, to get to the animals in time. And it was an all-too-rare stroke of luck when the father of a family came by with his children, pointed his finger at the hunger artist, gave a detailed explanation about what was going on here, and talked of earlier years, when he had been present at similar but incomparably more magnificent performances, and then the children, because they had been inadequately prepared at school and in life, always stood around still uncomprehendingly. What was fasting to them? But nonetheless the brightness of the look in their searching eyes revealed something of new and more gracious times coming. Perhaps, the hunger artist said to himself sometimes, everything would be a little better if his location were not quite so near the animal stalls. That way it would be easy for people to make their choice, to say nothing of the fact that he was very upset and constantly depressed by the stink from the stalls, the animals' commotion at night, the pieces of raw meat dragged past him for the carnivorous beasts, and the roars at feeding time. But he did not dare to approach the administration about it. In any case, he had the animals to thank for the crowds of visitors among whom, here and there, there could be one destined for him. And who knew where they

would hide him if he wished to remind them of his existence and, along with that, of the fact that, strictly speaking, he was only an obstacle on the way to the menagerie.

A small obstacle, at any rate, a constantly diminishing obstacle. People got used to the strange notion that in these times they would want to pay attention to a hunger artist, and with this habitual awareness the judgment on him was pronounced. He might fast as well as he could — and he did — but nothing could save him any more. People went straight past him. Try to explain the art of fasting to anyone! If someone doesn't feel it, then he cannot be made to understand it. The beautiful signs became dirty and illegible. People tore them down, and no one thought of replacing them. The small table with the number of days the fasting had lasted, which early on had been carefully renewed every day, remained unchanged for a long time, for after the first weeks the staff grew tired of even this small task. And so the hunger artist kept fasting on and on, as he once had dreamed about in earlier times, and he had no difficulty succeeding in achieving what he had predicted back then, but no one was counting the days — no one, not even the hunger artist himself, knew how great his achievement was by this point, and his heart grew heavy. And when once in a while a person strolling past stood there making fun of the old number and talking of a

swindle, that was in a sense the stupidest lie which indifference and innate maliciousness could invent, for the hunger artist was not being deceptive — he was working honestly — but the world was cheating him of his reward.

Many days went by once more, and this, too, came to an end. Finally the cage caught the attention of a supervisor, and he asked the attendant why they had left this perfectly useful cage standing here unused with rotting straw inside. Nobody knew, until one man, with the help of the table with the number on it, remembered the hunger artist. They pushed the straw around with a pole and found the hunger artist in there.

"Are you still fasting?" the supervisor asked. "When are you finally going to stop?"

"Forgive me everything," whispered the hunger artist. Only the supervisor, who was pressing his ear up against the cage, understood him.

"Certainly," said the supervisor, tapping his forehead with his finger in order to indicate to the spectators the state the hunger artist was in, "we forgive you."

"I always wanted you to admire my fasting," said the hunger artist.

"But we do admire it," said the supervisor obligingly.

"But you shouldn't admire it," said the hunger artist.

"Well then, we don't admire it," said the supervisor,

"but why shouldn't we admire it?"

"Because I had to fast. I can't do anything else," said the hunger artist.

"Just look at you," said the supervisor, "why can't you do anything else?"

"Because," said the hunger artist, lifting his head a little and, with his lips pursed as if for a kiss, speaking right into the supervisor's ear so that he wouldn't miss anything, "because I couldn't find a food which I enjoyed. If had found that, believe me, I would not have made a spectacle of myself and would have eaten to my heart's content, like you and everyone else."

Those were his last words, but in his failing eyes there was the firm, if no longer proud, conviction that he was continuing to fast.

"All right, tidy this up now," said the supervisor. And they buried the hunger artist along with the straw. But in his cage they put a young panther. Even for a person with the dullest mind it was clearly refreshing to see this wild animal throwing itself around in this cage, which had been dreary for such a long time. It lacked nothing. Without thinking about it for any length of time, the guards brought the animal food. It enjoyed the taste and never seemed to miss its freedom. This noble body, equipped with everything necessary, almost to the point of bursting, also appeared to carry freedom around with it.

That seem to be located somewhere or other in its teeth, and its joy in living came with such strong passion from its throat that it was not easy for spectators to keep watching. But they controlled themselves, kept pressing around the cage, and had no desire to move on.

二十世紀最偉大的捷克文學家：
作家生平解析

郭素芳／文字工作者

法蘭茲・卡夫卡
（Franz Kafka）

　　人分成很多種，天才也是。法蘭茲‧卡夫卡（Franz Kafka）無疑是那種心靈上最敏感纖細的天才。

　　生活上許多事物發生在平凡人的身上，如輕風撫過樹枝頭，對卡夫卡這樣的人卻不是，所有的事物如狂風橫掃過他的心靈國土，然後在狂風過後，他又需要時間一一將所有的事物細想後歸位。

　　這樣的人於一八八三年的七月三日誕生在今日捷克首都布拉格，當時是屬於奧匈帝國的波西米亞王國首府，整個政經文化深受奧地利與德國影響。一個需要安定與安全呵護並讓他自由創作的天才，卻要面對動盪的時代及一個由不同社會階層與觀念結合的家庭。

卡夫卡所處的時代背景

　　外在大環境方面，卡夫卡所面對的是世紀末動盪不安的政治變化，當時在哈布斯堡王朝統治下的奧匈帝國處於即將瓦解的邊緣，社會運動澎湃洶湧，西元一九一八年奧匈帝國經過第一次世界大戰的衝擊後解體，捷克與斯洛伐克共同組成捷克－斯洛伐克共和國，可是這個新生的國家並不安穩，衝突不斷。

　　除了政治動盪之外，布拉格人民的民族運動如排山倒海般對抗強勢的德意志文化，德裔與捷克裔之間對立衝突激烈，夾在兩者之間的少數猶太人只能在夾縫中求生存。卡夫卡的父親認同的是當時居主流社會階層的德國，因此他安排卡夫卡一路接受德文教育。卡夫卡的身份是如此複雜，他是個在布拉格出生長大說德語的猶太人。尤其甚者，當時傳統價值與文明受到強烈的質疑，尼采高呼上帝已死，新舊的思潮交互衝擊卡夫卡，於是，尋求個人存在價值、文化認同與思索民族定位便成了卡夫卡一生的課題。

父與子 —— 陽剛與陰柔的對立

對於卡夫卡而言，家庭環境的影響更甚於大環境。因為卡夫卡本身的性格是如此纖細敏感、順服溫柔，於是他的家庭才會是他心靈痛苦的根源。

這樣的人格特質大半來自母系基因的遺傳，卡夫卡的母親是尤莉·略維，她出身富裕，家族成員多數具有偏向心靈層面追求的獨特性格，從卡夫卡的外曾曾祖父到卡夫卡的舅公、舅舅，都有內向、古怪、害羞、安靜、固執、敏感等特徵，代代皆有學者與猶太教僧侶，卡夫卡的五個舅舅中有三個抱持獨身主義。

但是卡夫卡的父系家族卻與母系有著截然不同的性格，他們為了生活辛苦勞動，個個精力充沛，刻苦耐勞。尤其是卡夫卡的父親赫爾曼·卡夫卡，除了身材高大強壯外，他的意志堅強，固執強勢又有自信，重視生活上的實用價值，出身貧困卻白手起家建立起一個大公司，累積了巨額的財富。

五歲的卡夫卡

他這樣的人除了無法理解兒子之外，也無法諒解兒子。赫爾曼·卡夫卡對身為獨子的卡夫卡抱有莫大的期望，他希望卡夫卡以他為模範，繼承家業，期盼兒子像自己一樣剛猛，然而卡夫卡瘦弱的外表和內向的性格，與父親的期望完全不同，在赫爾曼·卡夫卡眼中，卡夫卡是個令人失望的兒子。

卡夫卡曾試圖告訴父親尊重與接受父子倆性格面的不同，沒有對錯或好壞，只是不同而已，他在寫給父親的一封信中提到，「將我們倆比較一下，我，簡而言之，是流著維略家族血液的卡

十歲的卡夫卡和兩個妹妹

夫卡：你才是一個眞正的卡夫卡，無論是強悍、健康、決斷力、能言善辯、耐力沉著等等無一不證明這點……相較之下，所有的這些在我身上幾乎都不存在……」可惜這封信並沒有交到父親手上，因爲母親知道父親看了這封信的反應只會使卡夫卡受到更大的傷害。

卡夫卡的父親

赫曼·卡夫卡
（Hermann Kafka，1852-1931）

卡夫卡在強勢的父親之前自信完全萎縮，他雖然生活在父親巨人般的陰影之下，卻仍深愛著父親與家庭，所以他不像一般人一樣選擇與父親決裂或離開。他痛苦地選擇成爲父親心目中的乖兒子，接受父親安排的路。

人生路上的知己

如果說卡夫卡最大的不幸是與父親不合，那麼卡夫卡人生的至幸便是在大學時認識了一生的摯友與知音—馬克斯·布勞德（Max Brod）。

布勞德也是猶太人，大一時與卡夫卡同修法律。他在一次文藝討論會上發表對叔本華與尼采的看法，極力抨擊卡夫卡喜愛的尼采是個「騙子」，散會後卡夫卡與他一同走路回家，爲各自的觀點辯論，之後，才發現對方也爲文學愛好者，自此結爲知交，惺惺相惜。

兩人經常一同參加文藝活動，討論文學與哲學，對當時的社會動盪發表看法，並參與彼此的生活，布勞德還寫信幫卡夫卡追女朋友。後來兩人開始走向創作之路，不過早早便發表作品出書的布勞德並不知道卡夫卡也在寫作（因爲卡夫卡從來不覺得寫作是爲了發表），直到卡夫卡朗讀了一段他寫的東西給布勞德聽，並將手稿交予他看之後，他才更加認識卡夫卡的才氣。

獨具慧眼的布勞德一眼就看出卡夫卡的不凡與天才，他看完卡夫卡作品後的感想是：「我既震驚又驚喜，並立即閃過一個念頭─這裡面顯現的不是一般的才能，而是天才！」從此布勞德不斷地鼓勵卡夫卡創作與發表著作，也極力向認識的出版商推薦卡夫卡的作品。他在一九一六年寫了一封信給編輯說：

> 我同時寄給您一篇卡夫卡的短篇作品，我花了比寫文章多十倍的時間，才從作者手上討來，要卡夫卡發表作品是極其困難的，要索取他的原稿簡直要用搶的！

看過卡夫卡作品的布勞德，這時也才真正地了解卡夫卡灰暗的內心世界，因為卡夫卡給他的印象一直是健康快樂、幽默風趣的。卡夫卡在朋友圈中並不多言，但是布勞德回憶說：「一旦他說起什麼，馬上會令人側耳傾聽，因為他的話總是內容充實，一語中的。與好友交談時，他的舌頭有時靈活得令人驚訝，甚至激越亢奮，直至忘我，風趣的話語和關懷的笑聲簡直無休無止。真的，他喜歡笑，笑得歡暢，也懂得如何逗朋友笑。還不止這樣，在困難的情況下，人們可以毫不猶豫地，放心地信賴他的通達事理、他的策略。作為朋友，他能奇妙的給予他人幫助，只有在處理自己的事情時，他才會束手無策，一籌莫展。」

布勞德更了解卡夫卡之後，對他的愛惜更甚，當卡夫卡陷入創作的瓶頸或生活上的憂鬱時，布勞德透過共同創作的方法引導卡夫卡繼續往前，也安排旅遊活動幫助擺脫鬱悶的日常生活。由於布勞德對卡夫卡的友愛，讓卡夫卡漸漸發展屬於自己的人生，並且將所有未發表的作品交予布勞德，要求在他死後把他所有作品焚燬。

當然，布勞德沒有遵照朋友的遺言，所以我們才有幸讀到《卡夫卡全集》和三部長篇小說：《審判》、《城堡》及《美國》。

這兩人的友誼讓我們知道所謂的文人相輕是因為那些文

人自信不足，無容人的雅量。布勞德是一個眞正的君子，卡夫卡何其有幸，世人何其有幸，給我們一個馬克斯‧布勞德。

職業與志業的掙扎

卡夫卡於一九〇六年取得法學博士，他拒絕接管家族企業已令父親失望，若無工作養活自己，在父母眼中更是沒出息，於是他經由舅舅的介紹先進入保險局擔任臨時雇員。爲了得到更多的時間來創作、看書、看戲、散步，他與布勞德積極尋覓工時較短的正式職業。後來卡夫卡進入「勞工事故保險局」工作，布勞德則進入郵政總局擔任法律顧問，兩人的下班時間都是午後兩點。

工作了一段時間後，兩人都發現打錯如意算盤了，因爲他們的工作十分痛苦乏味，分分秒秒對他們來說如歲歲年年般難熬。卡夫卡寫道：

> 辦公室對我來說是煩人的，經常是不可忍受的，但基本上又是容易應付的。透過這份工作，我所賺的錢遠超過我的需求。但，爲了什麼？爲了誰？我沿著薪資的梯子往上爬的意義何在？這

> 個工作不適合我，它從來不能給我帶來自立滿
> 足，只帶來工資……

除此之外，每天短暫的下午被太多瑣碎的事物分割，雖然卡夫卡嘗試利用各種方法去分配時間從事寫作，但最後總以失敗告終，因為卡夫卡需要一大段時間及安靜無噪音的空間，來捕捉他腦中的那個龐大世界，不容分割、干擾及打斷。

除了犧牲睡眠別無他法，他經常熬夜書寫，可是他的身體狀況不佳，缺乏睡眠令他身心俱疲。他在日記上寫著：

> 今天我正想起床，當下卻感到筋疲力竭。理
> 由很簡單，我太累了。這並不是辦公室造成的，
> 而是我的寫作。

他陷入了職業與志業的掙扎，職業只是一份工作，志業是發自靈魂深處所要從事的工作。卡夫卡不敢全心全意追求屬於自己生活。他像大部分的人一樣為了種種理由否定自我，將它鎖起來去當另一種人，過著另一種人生，也就是他父親認為正確的生活，而不照著自己的天賦本質發展。

布勞德認為卡夫卡最大的悲劇在於，像他這樣懷有豐富

才華與創作欲的天才，卻在生命力最旺盛的時期被迫日復一日地從事與內心毫不相干的事，直到筋疲力盡，引來疾病和死亡。

這世上有多少人穿著別人的鞋，追求屬於別人的路。

若即若離的愛情

卡夫卡雖終身未婚，但是他身邊的女性卻從來沒有斷過，他有一股強大的魔力使得許多女性對他著迷，也因他而心碎。

卡夫卡因布勞德的介紹而認識菲莉斯，他對她一見鍾情，寫信苦追佳人許久，又靠著布勞德的美言，才擄獲她的芳心。兩人交往了五年，但每當在論及婚嫁時，卡夫卡總對婚姻生活感到恐懼，而想要逃離。因為只要是與菲莉斯在一起時，他的寫作狀態就會中斷，他很愛菲莉斯但更愛寫作，寫作是他存在的依據。

我的生活基本上總是由寫作的嘗試構成，這絕大多數是失敗的嘗試。而一旦我不寫作，我就立刻被擊倒在地，像一堆垃圾……現在對您的思念豐富了我的生活。在我醒著的時候我幾乎沒有一刻不曾想過您，在許多這樣的一刻鐘內，我什麼也做不了。而即便這件事也與我的寫作有關。

卡夫卡寫給菲莉斯的信之信封

　　於是他擺盪在愛與不愛之間，渴望孤獨又想與人為伴，讓菲莉斯與自己飽受痛苦折磨。他曾經兩次與菲莉斯訂婚，卻又悔婚。後來，菲莉斯與柏林一位銀行家結婚，但終身保存卡夫卡寫給她的五百多封信。

　　同樣的情況也發生在尤麗葉身上，卡夫卡愛她戀她，但最後也與她解除婚約。

　　密倫娜則算是卡夫卡的紅顏知己，她因翻譯卡夫卡的作品而與卡夫卡結識相戀，她了解卡夫卡的恐懼，也由於這份了解而離開。

一直到後來，卡夫卡遇見了德國女友朵拉，所有的恐懼才全都消失。他第一次主動要求出版社出版他的作品，也找回了在父親之前枯萎的自信。他帶著朵拉搬到柏林去住，更計畫著與朵拉移民巴勒斯坦，展開全新的生活。可惜，死神早在門口等著他，他的病情惡化，讓深愛他的朵拉遭遇無比深沉的苦痛，最後更眼睜睜的看著他在病床前死去，而當時朵拉年僅二十歲。

卡夫卡對親情、愛情與婚姻既依賴又抗拒的矛盾掙扎，也許可以解釋為他的自私，他希望可以關起門來，無人干擾他寫作，卻又期盼一開門，一轉頭，朋友家人全都在他身旁。除非遇到真正適合又了解他的人，否則他只能陷於永不停止的痛苦中。

作品賞析

卡夫卡的作品是無國界的，只要社會不停往前邁進，一個人漸漸成長，遲早會與卡夫卡作品中的自己相遇。讀卡夫卡如遇知音。

你我就如同卡夫卡與他筆下的人物，在高度工業化、群體社會中尋找個體的定位。一開始人們依循傳統，以為努力賺錢，擁有許多物質享受後就會快樂，可是事實上問題接連不斷地到來，人的靈魂被自己所擁有的物質所束縛，無論是取得高成就者或所謂的失敗者，個體在群體中漸感孤立無援與疏離，在孤寂與焦慮感的重壓下，不停地尋找出口。思索這個問題的人逐漸匯集，他們提出的見解，人稱存在主義。

存在是指人的存在，人要選擇真正的自我，只有自覺的個人乃為真正的自我。存在主義主張反抗集體化的趨勢，強調個人必須過自己想要的生活，表達自己的思想，發揮自己的個性。

卡夫卡早我們一步面對這些問題，他的父母加諸在他身上的壓力、他面對職業選擇時的痛苦壓抑、他在現實生活中接收到的苦悶、對自我的懷疑，與腦中那個沒被禁錮，奇幻、想像與夢魘的世界連結後，卡夫卡給了我們一面鏡子去看看我們自己。

本書精選兩篇卡夫卡著名的短篇作品：〈變形記〉、〈飢餓藝術家〉，皆是深刻了解卡夫卡孤寂靈魂的窗口。

〈變形記〉

〈變形記〉是卡夫卡最出名的作品，他用寫實的手法表達出一種荒謬感，寫出普天下平凡上班族心中那股難以言喻的悲哀。

　　人一早醒來變成一隻與人身等長的大蟲，對卡夫卡及讀者來說彷彿是很正常的，沒什麼好奇怪的，好像只是生場怪病，起不來罷了。

　　一開始，變成蟲（生了病）的格勒果對於復原仍然抱持一點希望，因為他認為全家生計全靠他，因此非常關心變形之後父母與妹妹的生活，雖然骨子裡他十分痛恨推銷員的工作。諷刺的是，當格勒果無法外出賺錢之時，原本因破產喪志而無法工作的父親開始上班，身體虛弱的母親接了家庭手工，嬌生慣養的妹妹也出門當店員，連房子都分租給三個房客來貼補家用。格勒果為家庭所忍受的痛苦變得可笑，他存在的價值似乎消失了。漸漸地，他身為人的習性也慢慢消失，僅存人的思考與情感，卻無法與外界溝通。家人對他漸趨冷漠，到了後來甚至嫌惡他，他被父親用蘋果砸傷了背部，連同嵌在裡面的蘋果一起發爛，笨重身軀沾黏了食物殘屑與灰塵，孤獨地關在房間裡爬來爬去。後來，格勒果在妹妹演奏小提琴時，不知不覺地被琴音所吸引，而爬出房間，那三個房客看到他，憤怒地表示要退租。這件事讓格勒果的家人崩潰了，他們再也不願意忍受格勒果，他們說服自己那隻醜陋的大蟲並不是格勒果，希望他消失在他們眼前。

　　格勒果也認為他的離開對家人是最好的結果，於是虛弱受傷又許久未進食的格勒果在凌晨停止了呼吸。

《變形記》原著出版的封面

《變形記》首頁筆跡和卡夫卡親筆簽名

〈變形記〉的悲劇在於格勒果用痛苦的汁液去餵養心中關住的自我，他厭惡自己、工作與家庭，卻無力反抗，等到用痛苦毒汁餵食的自我逐漸成長，終於變形成蟲，衝破表層的假象。

〈飢餓藝術家〉

表演飢餓的藝術家剛開始巡迴歐洲表演時，人們觀賞的興致很高，藝術家所到之處萬人空巷，人們驚奇地圍在他的鐵籠前。他說飢餓表演是世上最容易的事，人們不了解他所說的話，以為他是謙虛或者吹牛。每一次飢餓表演的規定期限是四十天，藝術家對於這一點非常不滿，因為他的能力不僅止於此。

在表演事業最巔峰的時候，他一點都不覺得高興，反而陰鬱易怒，人們說那是因為他餓太久的關係。

飢餓表演後來不流行了，但他除了表演飢餓無法從事別的職業。藝術家告別了經紀人，加入一家馬戲團。在馬戲團裡，他表演的鐵籠子被安排在關野獸的籠子旁，人潮再度洶湧而至，不過並不是來看他的，而是為了去看那些兇猛的野獸，無人看他一眼。但藝術家依然認真地表演，而且確定這次一定會破紀錄，雖然沒人替他計算日期。

最後，連馬戲團的人都忘了他的存在，讓他自生自滅，直到有一天，管理員發現一個空著的鐵籠子，責怪員工竟浪費一個可以用的鐵籠子時，他們才想起飢餓藝術家，趕緊把奄奄一息的他從草堆中撈起來。管理員問他為什麼不停止表演去吃東西，臨死的藝術家對管理員說：

「我只能挨餓，我沒有別的辦法。我找不到適合自己口味的食物。如果我找得到，請相信我，我絕不會這樣驚動他人，會像你和大家一樣，吃得飽飽的。」

〈飢餓藝術家〉是卡夫卡最珍愛的短篇之一，死前一天他還在病床上校對以〈飢餓藝術家〉為書名的短篇作品集。

此篇作品表達了卡夫卡的心聲與吶喊。飢餓藝術家在飢餓中生活，恰如卡夫卡在寫作中生活，對他而言這是非常容易的，並不像人們所以為的那麼困難。他很願意過一般人的生活，只是怎麼樣都找不到屬於自己真實存在的意義，他不得不在寫作中尋找自我，如果他在現實生活中能夠如一般大眾一樣找到自我的定位，那他也會與大家一樣吃得飽飽、活得好好的。

藝術家與卡夫卡卻不被世人所了解，不論是喜歡他或漠視他的人都一樣。人們只以自己的觀點去解釋他人的行為與想法。

卡夫卡的素描

國家圖書館出版品預行編目資料

卡夫卡變形記 / 法蘭茲‧卡夫卡（Franz Kafka）作；
李毓昭譯. -- 臺中市：晨星，2019.10
　　面；　公分. --（愛藏本；98）
中英雙語典藏版
譯自：The Metamorphosis
ISBN 978-986-443-912-6（精裝）

882.457　　　　　　　　　　　　　108011879

愛藏本：98

卡夫卡變形記（中英雙語典藏版）
The Metamorphosis

作者｜法蘭茲·卡夫卡（Franz Kafka）
繪者｜楊宛靜
譯者｜李毓昭

責任編輯｜呂曉婕
封面設計｜鐘文君
美術設計｜黃偵瑜
文字校潤｜呂曉婕

填寫線上回函，立刻享有
晨星網路書店50元購書金

創辦人｜陳銘民
發行所｜晨星出版有限公司
　　　　台中市 407 工業區 30 路 1 號 1 樓
　　　　TEL:(04)23595820　FAX:(04)23550581
　　　　http://star.morningstar.com.tw
　　　　行政院新聞局版台業字第 2500 號
法律顧問｜陳思成律師
初版日期｜2019 年 10 月 01 日
再版日期｜2023 年 02 月 15 日（三刷）
　　ISBN｜978-986-443-912-6
　　定價｜新台幣 250 元

讀者服務專線｜TEL：02-23672044 / 04-23595819#212
讀者傳真專線｜FAX：02-23635741 / 04-23595493
讀者專用信箱｜E-mail：service@morningstar.com.tw
　　網路書店｜https://www.morningstar.com.tw
　　郵政劃撥｜15060393（知己圖書股份有限公司）

印刷｜上好印刷股份有限公司